AFRAID

ALPHA'S LITTLE PSYCHO
BOOK 3

K.A. BAUER

Afraid (Alpha's Little Psycho 3)
Cover Artwork by K.A. Bauer
Copyright © 2023 K.A. Bauer
All Rights Reserved

Paperback ISBN 979-8-9892840-6-1

CIP data for the individual books are available from the Library of Congress

❋ Created with Vellum

TRIGGER WARNING

PLEASE DO NOT PROCEED IF YOU ARE NOT COMFORTABLE WITH THESE ELEMENTS. YOUR MENTAL HEALTH IS MORE IMPORTANT THAN MY BOOK SALES.

Please be advised that this book contains mention or depiction of the following elements which may be upsetting or triggering to some readers.

BDSM

AGE PLAY

CHILD ABUSE AND NEGLECT

SEXUAL ASSAULT

TRAFFICKING

PTSD FLASHBACKS

BULLYING

SUICIDAL IDEATIONS

EXTREME VIOLENCE

EXPLICIT LANGUAGE

AFRAID

ALPHA'S LITTLE PSYCHO BOOK 3

PROLOGUE

40 Years Ago

"Esther, baby? I need you to take this letter over to Mrs. Sinclair." Mommy's voice rings out from the kitchen. Ever since she started growing my baby sister in her belly, she's been acting strange. She doesn't spend any time with us anymore because she's always tired. I guess growing babies is hard work, but I don't remember her being this tired with Carl. Then again, I was only four when my little brother came around...

"Sweetie? It's important!"

"Coming, Mama," I call back, dragging my feet.

I don't know what could be so important that she needs to send something over to the Beta's mate and not call her over here. Daddy says we're a special family from a very important bloodline and this pack should be happy to have us. He says I'm going to be the one to bring our bloodline back into power since Alpha Alistair has a son around my age. I'm not sure what Daddy means, but I like Ricky. I am looking forward to being his mate someday...

Grabbing the letter from the counter, I call out a goodbye to my mom and my little brother and race towards the big house that the Sinclairs live in. It's pretty enough, but it's nothing like the Alpha house, the pack house. I'm destined for greatness and deserve nothing less. That's what Daddy says.

When I come up to the little pond, I stop to sit for a bit. This is my happy place. It's almost like no one knows about it. It's a little secret for me... While I'm sitting, I glance at the envelope in my hand...

Who is Edward Sullivan? Why is Mama writing to a strange man?

I know it's naughty, but I open the letter and start to read. I'm eight, almost nine, and I am very advanced for my age. Daddy says I'm a genius...

I can't understand some of the words I'm reading, but I see enough...Mama wants to leave. Mama wants to take me away from Daddy, from my future with Ricky, from my destiny...

NO!

I stuff the paper back in the envelope and hide it under a rock. That will show this Edward person. He won't ever know to come back for Mama, so we won't have to leave Daddy. I don't even care about the words that my sister isn't Daddy's as long as we stay together. I won't leave Daddy. I am his princess and I'm supposed to do great things for this pack...

Daddy says so.

6 *Months Later*

I miss Mama.

Daddy figured out that Elizabeth's daddy is not him and he got really mad at Mama. He sent me and Carl out of the house that day, but when we came home, Mama was gone and Elizabeth was here. Daddy says Mama died because of what Elizabeth is, because her daddy wasn't him and the Goddess punished Mama for her infidelamy or something like that. I forgot to look up the word.

But it's all *his* fault, that Edward man Mama was writing to. Daddy says so. Now, I'm nine and the lady of the Welling household and it's more important than ever to be proper and dignified and bring the honor to our family that I'm supposed to. Daddy says it's time for me to be grown and sponsible.

I can't cry about Mama in front of Daddy without making him angry. He says to the world, we need to make sure everyone thinks that Elizabeth's daddy is him so that people don't think badly of Mama. I'm a big girl now. It's my job to protect the family reputation.

Sitting on the stoop to get away from my sleeping sister, a strange car pulls up. I don't know who it could be, but they better not wake the baby. She's very loud when she first wakes up, and I have a headache from crying again.

The man who gets out of the car looks a little familiar. I can't figure out where I've seen him before. Then, he asks for Mama...

I remember him now. He's the stupid head who caused Mama to go away. He wanted to take us away from Daddy. I yell at him and tell him Mama's gone. Somehow, I slip up and tell him only me and Carl are really Wellings, but Daddy will forgive me for one slip up, right? To everyone else, she'll be my one hundred percent little sister...

The man looks really really sad when he gets back into his car. I don't like him being sad, but he has to go away. He wanted to take Mama and if he stays, he's going to try and take my sister. She belongs here. She belongs with me.

It's hours after the man drives off, but I'm back on the stoop, on the lookout for him to try and come back to take my baby sister away. While I'm waiting, Johnny Sinclair comes out of the woods and sits next to me. He's kinda cute for a teenager, but Daddy says I have to mate with Ricky when I turn eighteen. Maybe he'll even be my true mate...

"Penny for your thoughts?" Johnny asks me, nudging my shoulder with his own.

"I miss Mama," I tell him honestly. I can't reveal what happened earlier, but it's true that if Mama was still here, I could just be a regular little girl again.

"Speaking of your mom," he says looking into the trees. "I found a letter from her addressed to someone in South Carolina about a week ago. When I showed my mom, she had me race it to the post office. You know anything about that?"

My blood freezes in my veins.

How did Johnny find the letter?

How was it even still in one piece?

I hid it so good.

"Did you read it?" I ask, dreading the answer. Daddy says no one can know.

Johnny shakes his head and I feel like I can breathe again. I don't mean to let them out, but I can feel some stray tears fall from my eyes. He puts his arm around me and pulls me close. I don't really understand why he's being so nice, but I'll take it. It feels really nice to get a hug again.

9 Years Later

"Richard has met his fated mate! I won't split them up!"

I don't usually argue with my father, but this time he's gone too far. Fated mates are sacred. Annabelle is a scared little mouse, but apparently the fates gave her to Richard, our future Alpha. Dad is just angry that they found each other before I turned eighteen. Not my fault I can't control when I was born...

"Fine then. If you won't push for an Alpha, you'll mate with the future Beta!"

Wait... what? He wants me to mate with Johnny?

"Dad, he's almost twenty five now! Don't I even get a chance to find my fated one?"

"You are my daughter!" he screams at me. "You don't get choices. You do what you're told for the good of this family!"

I storm up the steps to my room and slam the door. Collapsing on my bed, I use my pillows to muffle the sobs I can't hold back any longer. When did I stop being his princess and become a freaking piece of property to sell off? How am I supposed to reach my destiny if I can't be with my fated mate? How did Anna end up with my destiny, anyway?

When a small hand taps my shoulder, I startle. I didn't even hear the door open, but the little twit has always been silent. She's had to be with the way Dad's temper has been...

"Sissy?" Lizzie looks a bit scared, so I hurriedly wipe at my eyes. She doesn't know how lucky she is that she isn't blood related to that drunk downstairs. Even though he's cruel to her behind closed doors, at least she doesn't have to worry about ending up like him.

"It's okay, sweetie," I whisper as I pull her into my lap. "Everything will be okay."

7 Years Later

The Heartstone Alpha and his son have finally left. That was the longest three months ever.

When they arrived, suddenly my mate and the Alpha were needed to be locked up in meetings all day every day. That left me to deal with two toddler boys who just wanted to get into everything possible.

Anna was useless as usual. She's nothing more than arm candy to Richard... a disgrace to she-wolves everywhere.

And then Liz just up and disappeared for most of the time they were here.

I caught her with Bennet a few times, but I didn't say anything. I mean, the secret's out that my mother had an affair, thanks to Liz not getting a wolf, and all. But behind closed doors, she's still my precious little sister. I have to put up a front when Father is around or else deal with his anger issues. Most of the time, those are focused on her now. I still feel the need to protect her and keep her with me, so I allow her to help me with Connor and Alaric. She belongs with me. She's safe with me.

At least now things are getting back to normal with the visitors gone. Liz is helping me out with watching the boys again while I keep the house clean and plan the parties and events. This is the way our pack is run. This is how I get to be the most important she-wolf in the Jameson pack. Alistair let it slip that Richard is likely to not be the next Alpha, so it looks like the Sinclairs will be moving up... the Goddess really has blessed me after all.

6 Months Later

"Elizabeth Welling! You tell me who it was before I rip that bastard out myself!"

I race into the living room to see my father looming over my baby sister. Today is her sixteenth birthday. We are supposed to be having a girls day, so that I could pamper her. Pregnancy isn't easy, and I need her to get through it so that she can go back to watching Connor again.

I was hoping she wouldn't provoke Father today and have at least one day without a beating from him. It's been a regular occurrence since she started to show. She hasn't told anyone who the father is, but I'm pretty sure it was Bennet. When I asked her, she just said she doesn't want anyone else to know until she can tell him herself.

I've tried to reach out to him discreetly, but his father is keeping him isolated within their pack. Alpha Heartstone just keeps saying that his son cannot be in contact with known vampire sympathizers or something. I can't tell him he's going to be a father unless Liz confirms it's him because I don't want to start an incident between packs if it turns out I'm wrong...

"I know what you did to my mother," Liz growls breaking through my thoughts. I've never heard that kind of a tone from her before. She's my sunshine girl. She doesn't DO angry. "You killed our mother because she had me and wanted to take us away from you! You were more concerned for your reputation than the health and well-being of your mate! You went against FATE for your own selfish reasons!"

The force of his slap sends Liz flying across the room. I watch as her body collides with the dining room table and crumples to the floor, not moving. Kneeling beside her I see she is still breathing, but there is blood pooling between her legs.

I hesitate.

I know it's wrong and my niece or nephew doesn't deserve to suffer, but I want my sister back. I want her whole and healthy and all of her love directed at me again...

If I can't have her back, then she should just get to be at peace with Mama and her baby and not have to face this cruel world anymore... She shouldn't have to face Father's wrath anymore and this will allow us to get rid of him as well. Alistair will never let him remain alive after this...

Carl and I can be free... Liz can be free... We'll all be better off this way.

I grab my father and drag him from the house, locking the door behind me. Getting into the car, I head for Dayton. It's time to get him good and fully drunk so that I can get rid of him once and for all. I'm going to miss my sister, but this is the best outcome for everyone.

7 Hours Later

John dropped off Connor with me about three hours ago. He said something about the Alpha and an emergency visitor. I wasn't really listening. I had just finished dragging my father's sorry ass to his bedroom. Three hundred dollars of liquor wasted on that sorry excuse of a man, just to get the cover story of him being drunk and pushing her into the table. I can't afford to have him remember I was there.

After all, my family can't have a bad reputation...

It's after ten at night before my mate comes home. I had to do the whole bedtime routine with Connor by myself. I hate having to tuck him in, but it's much better now that he's in kindergarten and mostly self sufficient. I'm going to have to get used to not having Liz around to take care of him...

"Esther? Can you come to the living room?"

I put down my book and sigh. It's so unfair that I ended up with the older and responsible mate. John is objectively good looking and all, but he's so boring. Ricky and I are a much better match, but he picked Anna the waif and left me with the grandpa.

Walking into the room, I'm surprised to see John is not alone. Alpha Alistair is here along with Richard and another man who has his back to me. When the stranger turns around, I feel as if I've turned to ice. It's *him*...

"Hello again, Esther," he says to me looking up from the bundle in his arms.

Oh, no... The baby survived. He knows everything...

He keeps talking and talking but my brain isn't computing. Terror has a stranglehold on my comprehension abilities. The only thing I'm hearing is my heartbeat pounding away like it knows it's about to stop any second. John is just nodding along and takes the baby into his arms as if nothing is wrong.

Wait a second... Why is my mate taking the baby?

"I think it would be good if family raises him, at least until he gets his wolf," John says while Alistair shakes his head in agreement.

Family? Does John expect *me* to raise another child? How would this look to the rest of the pack? Raising my sister's bastard kid...

I wish I could have Lizzie here to do it. She did everything when Connor was a baby. I don't know anything about babies. I never even changed a diaper! Give him to someone else since she's not around, not me!

"He will be a Sinclair until you come to claim him, King Edward."

King?

My wolf speaks up for the first time in years to smugly say, *If you hadn't shut me out I could have told you that your sister wasn't a human halfling, but vampire. You have been connected to royalty but it will never benefit you. You are nothing. Your greed and narcissism will always be your downfall.*

I slam the door shut on her again in my mind. There is a reason I don't let her out anymore. She questions everything I do. She says I'm wrong. I know I'm not wrong. I am the one responsible for my house. I am the most important she-wolf in the pack...

Almost 5 Years Later

The little shit is running again. There's only so much cleaning I can force on a four year old. I'm not worried about over exerting him or anything. He just can't reach shit yet. I can't wait for him to get older so that people will stop thinking he's cute and will see him for the disrespectful bastard that he is. Vampire princeling... bullshit. He's a waste of oxygen.

The thud followed by a whimper makes my blood boil. I hate the sound of his whimpers. If Connor is around, the world stops when Ethan is upset. Connor has more important things to worry about. He needs to be focused on maintaining his friendship with Alaric, not worrying about this *thing* he believes is his brother.

The sight of the blood on the carpet when I walk into the room sets my teeth on edge. Why did he have to bleed? Now, I have to call the doctor...

After the doctor shows up, I am ready to leave them be and get back to my book. But then the doctor scolds me for wasting his time... Me? Why in the fuck am I getting treated like a child?

Does he not know who I am?

Then his words register... there is no wound. I've been researching halflings and hybrids for years now ever since finding out my beloved little sister was one. Ethan shouldn't have healing abilities like this at four... not as a wolf and not as a vampire, so how?

I drag him to my secret room in the basement. John knows I reorganized the wine cellar, but has no clue that my "personal space" is actually my office for my research. I'm working on converting part of it into a lab for experiments. I may not have the degrees to back it up, but I do have a fascination with genetics, biology, and anatomy... Looking down at the simpering welp in front of me, I believe I just found the perfect test subject.

3 *Weeks Later*

"Are you fucking insane, woman!?"

Richard is not reacting the way I expected him to. This is the only possible solution. I didn't know about the blood oath until Anna mentioned something. She made a comment after seeing a bruise on Ethan's neck yesterday. Apparently, Alistair is sworn to punish anyone who harms Ethan.

I need my test subject, so the logical answer is to eliminate Alistair...

"I've already set the story, Ricky. You just have to do the deed," I tell him. "No one will suspect you and you'll finally get everything you wanted."

Richard doesn't stop pacing in front of me. I probably shouldn't be staring at his dick swinging back and forth as he turns, but it's hard not to look. We've been together regularly since we were both twenty. After Alaric was born, Anna decided she didn't want any more kids. Without his so-called mate clouding his choices, Ricky came back to me. He loves me. He's always loved only me.

"I can't just kill my father to save your ass," he growls at me.

"What about your own?" I ask him. "Your father has already decided to skip over you for the title of Alpha and give it to Alaric when he turns twenty one. He's sworn it to the Goddess. You will be nothing!"

After a moment of shock, Richard shifts to his wolf and takes off through the open window. The sight of the powerful chocolate wolf always makes me sigh...

Now, I get to set the stage for a "vampire attack" and make

sure that Ethan gets some sort of blame for it all. It's unfortunate that a few other pups will have to die, but it's a sacrifice that needs to be made... for the future of my family and this pack.

8 Years Later

Ethan turned thirteen today and John dragged us out to the disgusting little pond on the property to witness his first shift. I was honestly hoping he would not shift at all, like Liz, and then the pack would completely ostracize him... but yet again the little shit found a way to piss me off by succeeding.

Not only does Ethan have a wolf, but he's moonlight silver... and his eyes didn't change. Through my research, I discovered only one bloodline has these traits. Only the firstborn son of the Heartstone pack is able to be the color of the moon while retaining his human eyes. This means, I was right. Liz got knocked up by Bennet Heartstone, and we've been harboring the heir to his pack for the last thirteen years.

Oh, but it gets better... Richard let it drop to me last night that he promised Ethan to the fae once he gained his wolf, so now our Alpha has sold the son of another Alpha to the fae.

Then you add in the fact that Alaric, the Alpha heir, is over-protective with the mongrel.. Oh and did I forget to mention the little bastard presents as an omega as well?

Why am I cursed like this? What did I ever do to deserve this?

Then, my little brother did something extremely stupid. My brother is an idiot most of the time, but this time he out-did himself. He runs in some questionable circles, but he decided to try and cut out the Alpha and sell Ethan to a *human* lab. Human! Like, I get that the money is good, especially since we discovered he's omega, but one of the cardinal freaking rules is to hide ourselves from humans...

Nowhere in these plans did anyone consult me... the brains of the operations. I swear I have more brain cells in my pinky finger than they all have combined.

Did they all just forget that his grandfather, the mother-fucking King of the vampires, is supposed to be coming back for him?

Now, I'm stuck planning cleanup of everything. I had to call in a favor with a fae acquaintance that I didn't want to cash in to buy some time with the vampire. The dispute will be cleared up quickly, but I only needed to delay him for a day.

I finally hear silence from the end of the house where the boys' rooms are. At least I made sure Connor and Alaric are not going to be around for tonight. Ricky will get rid of Ethan with the fae and we'll cover our tracks and Carl will just have to go without a payday. The plan is already in place.

Shouting from downstairs pulls me from the office. I just finished setting up the email to send to Edward in the morning. I had already sent the obligatory birthday one this afternoon. I've gotten really good at photoshop over the years for the pictures. This email will mention Ethan's death by fire. Hopefully, it will keep him away long enough to find a body to use.

I'm surrounded by idiots... they don't know how to look at the whole picture like I do. That's why they should have consulted me. I am a genius after all...

The sweet smell of a sedative overtakes me before I can even get up from the desk. I know it because I'm the one who developed this one to work on the abomination. His healing abilities nullify anything else within a few minutes unless it's continually admin-istered.

Damnit, Carl! What the fuck have you done?!

When I come back to myself, I'm tied up tight in my bed with some sort of vines. It has to be hours later. John is beside me, but he's not tied up, though. Why wouldn't they tie him up? I stare at him looking for a sign that he's coming around, but the realization comes too late. There is no heartbeat. He is not breathing. My mate is dead...

"You have broken the deal," says a reedy voice from the shadows. "Let the flames purify your wicked, lying soul."

The fae are here? If the deal is broken, that means Carl actually stole the boy and cut us all out!

I try speak to let them know who has their prize. No sound can come out. This isn't right! I did nothing wrong!

I try to scream in frustration and rage as flames erupt at the foot of the bed, creeping up to tickle my feet. I try and try as the pain rips into my flesh, but the only sound to be heard above the roar of the flames is a cackling laughter from the corner.

"Goodbye, Esther Welling-Sinclair. You've earned your spot in hell."

Agreed, whispers my wolf as the blackness of oblivion overtakes the flames...

ONE

Ethan

It takes me a few moments to figure out where I am when I wake up. The events of the last few months have made life a bit unpredictable. I went from being an unwanted bastard orphan to being the son of an Alpha and grandson of a vampire king... Oh and let's not forget that I'm also part fae, an omega, and fucking pregnant...

WITH TWINS!

As if my life wasn't difficult enough so far, let's just add in another major fucking obstacle to any chance of me ever being happy. Every single time I think I might be able to finally let go and just be happy, fate goes and just flips the bird and rips it all away again.

First, my mother dies in childbirth. Apparently, I was fucking up people's lives before I was even born to the point I managed to take out the *one* person who is supposed to love me without a reason to. Then, I'm given to a sadistic bitch who let me believe that she was my mother. I spent thirteen years of my life trying to get a single smile from her, a single word of praise...anything but contempt and violence...

As if that wasn't bad enough, practically the entire pack tried to kill me from the time I was in kindergarten, maybe earlier. I don't really remember. All I know is that as long as it could be ruled an accident, no one got in trouble for hurting me. None of the adults stopped it. Most of the other kids ignored it. I was so happy to get my wolf because at least with him, there was a way to escape if I ever got up the courage...

But then I was kidnapped and sold to a lab. I used to think my Uncle Carl did it for the dickwad that was our Alpha, but no... that wasn't the case. He did it for money. Alpha Richard wanted to give me to the fae to save his own ass cuz he couldn't keep it in his pants and was cut out of the deal and fucked over when Uncle Carl sold me for fifty grand to some asswipe in rural Ohio for experiments.

How fucked is that? I was sold off like an old vase. Actually, old vases are treated better than I was during transport... But people died because of that night, not like it mattered to the assholes who bought and sold me. They just wanted their money, their freedom. I almost wish those selfish pricks hadn't died so that I could get some sort of revenge...

We survived. We have mate. We have pups.

I don't want to hear my wolf right now. Yeah. I survived. I *always* survive. I can't die unless I lose my heart or my head completely. Yet another thing to curse my existence...

I stare at the ceiling of the bedroom I share with Ric and wish, not for the first time, that I had died in that lab... and stayed dead. If I had, everyone would be happy. No one would be worried or scared...

I wouldn't be terrified...

I've started feeling the little flutters in my belly. They're real now. I can't pretend anymore. I have two lives inside of me that are going to depend on me to keep them safe. But I am going to leave them even though I don't want to. My mother died in childbirth. My grandmother died in childbirth. It's going to happen to me, too. I just know it.

Ric isn't ready to be a father by himself just yet. I need to make sure everything is ready for them all to get by without me. I really don't want to leave, but...

My hand brushes the scar on my throat that still hasn't completely healed. I have the feeling it's not going to ever go away. There's something about my being pregnant that allowed me to scar, I'm sure of it. The papercut from three days ago hasn't healed. I don't heal correctly when I'm pregnant...

My phone rings and snaps me out of my thoughts. I can hear Ric curse from downstairs. I can only imagine he meant to either turn off my ringer or take my phone down with him to his office. Looking at the screen, I see it's Shaun calling. I answer so that Ric doesn't think I'm still asleep and I'll get at least some privacy for this conversation. After I say hello, I hear the click of the office door closing... yep, privacy.

"Hey, E-man," Shaun says softly. He's been gentle with me these last two months. I still can't bring myself to go into the hospital after everything that's happened, so he's had to rely on only his witchy senses to help me with my pregnancy.

"How are the twins doing today? Any weird cravings yet?"

I think about it and realize that aside from the one or two days of morning sickness, the flutters are the only real symptom I've had. Hearing that, Shaun seems to be happier than he was when he first started talking. Even though he's acting as my baby doctor, I want to talk to my best friend, so I change the subject to one that will get attention off of me.

"How's my brother treating you? Still waking up to presents on the porch?"

I had to miss the fireworks, but my best friend and my big brother discovered they're fated mates. Shaun apparently rejected Connor, but my brother is being stubborn, rightly so... I want my family whole and together and happy when I'm gone.

My voice barely wobbles as I continue the conversation, listening to my bestie going on and on about how he doesn't need another carcass or fur or blanket or groceries or anything else from my brother. It's been over six weeks and Connie's wolf seems convinced he can win over his mate while Connie himself is turning into a hermit.

Hanging up the call after about an hour of useless chit chat, I decide to go to my playroom down the hall. I'm not feeling particularly little lately, especially as my belly grows, but I want to cuddle with more than Mr. Whiskers and get away from being a grownup for a while. No one questions me or expects anything of me when I'm in my playroom. Only my stuffies know how I really feel about it all.

Ric

Something has been bothering my boy since he came back, and it's only getting worse. My Beta is in a state of mourning over his mate while his wolf is still attempting to court them. My head warrior disappears regularly, coming back more and more reserved and angry each time. Even my little brother is more emotional than usual.

Ever since our parents died, Jackie has been surrounded by me, Connor, and Max. We are the constants in his life... his whole life...

In the last year, since we found out Ethan was alive, everything has changed. We added Ethan, and Jack practically worships him. But since we got him back this time and started preparing for the twins, it's like a cloud of fear has settled on everything.

I'm terrified of losing my mate. I can't forget the fact that his healing doesn't work when he's pregnant. I asked Bennet about it last month when Ethan got a splinter that took over three hours to heal. He's just as clueless as I am. The curse, or blessing, has never fallen on an omega so we're in uncharted territory. The only theory we have is that the healing is split between father and babies since they cannot protect themselves.

All of us are looking into it, researching everything we can. I've even gotten over my aversion to Edward... mostly. The healing thing might be vampire related after all and we can't leave any stone unturned. The vampire said he'll look into it and get back to us. That was three days ago, and I'm just pacing in my office waiting for the phone to ring, like I've been for two and a half days.

A phone does ring, breaking the silence, but it's coming from our bedroom.

Shit... I forgot to grab Ethan's phone. He's supposed to be resting and relaxing according to Shaun. Until we can get him to do an ultrasound, we can only rely on Shaun's knowledge and witchcraft to help keep track of the babies and Ethan's health.

Before I manage to exit my office, I hear my boy answer the phone. He sounds like he's fully awake, so I decide he should enjoy his conversation. With Connor and Max being absent so much and Jack still in school for the next few weeks, Ethan needs a bit of interaction aside from me.

Turning back towards the desk, I feel my phone vibrate in my pocket. I pull it out and see "Gramps the Vamp" on the screen... My boy got into my phone again...

"Gimme a second, Edward," I say as I answer, still chuckling. I listen for a second out in the hallway to make sure my boy is still on the phone before I close the door to my office. This needs to be a private conversation. I don't want to worry my bluebird if I don't have to.

"Ok, we've got privacy," I tell him when I've settled into my desk chair.

"I've been looking into it, but vampire omegas are extremely rare, so we don't have much to go on," he starts off with a sigh. This isn't looking up. I don't like not knowing the dangers my mate is facing.

"But, as my wonderful sister-in-law reminded me, it's not only omegas that give birth," he adds with a chuckle. "Female vampires need to *suspend* their immortality in order to conceive apparently. This makes them as vulnerable as humans while they are pregnant according to her. This is also why you never see a pregnant vampire ..."

My brain falters for a moment while I try to compute what he's saying. If it's his vampire blood halting his healing, how in the hell am I supposed to protect him? He would never let me lock him away for his own safety.

"... as Seamus discovered, it doesn't really help."

I missed something more to the story and have to ask him to repeat himself. As I thought, vampires don't like to be coddled and it would definitely create an issue with my mate. We end up going back and forth for over two hours trying to come up with ways to protect Ethan without smothering him, and in the end it doesn't even matter.

Ethan will always do whatever he thinks is best for everyone but himself. Our biggest challenge is going to be to get him to remember the babies before he acts on anything...

I am finally able to leave my office after another hour. I had to sign off on all of the financial stuff that Connor usually handles. My Beta had better get his act together soon... especially before the babies get here. I'm not going to be an absentee father like mine was just because my best friend can't figure out his romantic life.

Once I reach the top of the stairs, I can pinpoint that my boy is in his playroom. I hear him talking to his stuffies. It's been a while since I've seen my little boy Blue come out to play and I can't fight the grin that starts to spread on my face. I didn't realize how much I miss being Daddy...

"They don't need to be scared like me so you gotta promise me you won't tell Daddy or Max or Connie or even Jackie, okay guys? Bertie, I'm talking to you, too!"

I stop just outside the door. He hasn't noticed my approach at all. My heart is splintering into a million pieces... he's afraid...

Now the question is, what is he afraid of? Is it the same fear I have for his healing? Or does he know something I don't?

TWO

Ethan

Something has changed with Ric over the last few weeks. I mean, it's nice to have my Daddy spoiling me all of the time, but he's taking it to the extreme.

I don't think I really need to get breakfast in bed every morning.

I really don't think I need to have catered meals from a nutritionist for every dinner.

I don't think I need to have a mini fridge and snack station in my playroom... Okay I actually really like this development, but the point remains.

It's almost like he doesn't want me to go downstairs...

Shaun throws a stuffie at my head and snaps me out of my thoughts.

"What is the plan for tomorrow?" he asks me when I throw Cecil back at him. The demon kitty misses by a mile of course. My aim is much better with knives and other sharp and pointies.

It takes a minute for me to remember what tomorrow even is... May twenty third, my birthday. I turn twenty two tomorrow.

It's also the anniversary of both my mother and grandmother's deaths.

I didn't really need the reminder. Today was the first day in at least a week that I didn't wake up in a panic because I'm not ready to say goodbye.

I don't want tomorrow to come.

I'm not ready to die...

I didn't even notice the panic attack until I feel my Daddy's arms wrapped around me from behind. Looking down, I see his legs stretched out on either side of me and I'm sitting on the floor. The strangeness of it helps pull me back to reality a bit more.

I don't sit on the floor anymore. At almost five months pregnant with twins, if I get on the floor, I can't get back up on my own.

"...tomorrow could be a trigger?" I hear from Shaun.

I'm half clued into their conversation, but I'm also distracted by Max in the doorway. I don't understand the look on his face. He's so tired. It looks like he hasn't had a good night's sleep in at least a month.

Daddy needs to put his foot down and give him time off.

Daddy's gonna need him real soon...

Blue? You back with us, baby?

Daddy is talking in my head. I don't have much control over my abilities since I got pregnant, so Shaun has helped me build a wall to hold it all in so I'm not leaking my brain stuff on everyone. But they can all still talk to me.

It's like a one way thing right now, which is good. I don't want to worry them all more than they already are.

Sweetheart?

I turn my head and look at Ric. I need to pull back a bit from thinking of him as my Daddy. He needs to be ready to be Dada, not Daddy now. There's no real way to reassure him if I try to open my mouth. I'm barely holding back the screams as it is.

I have less than twenty four hours to get everything ready.

The look in his eyes is ripping my heart to shreds. I can see the pain and the worry growing. I need to make him happy. I need this last day to be a happy day, so I stretch as much as I can to plant a kiss on his chin - I can't reach his cheek from here.

I have to turn back around quickly or he'll see, he'll know...

I can feel Daddy's chuckle as he holds me tighter and plants a responding kiss to the top of my head. I think I pulled it off.

One last good day with Daddy...

My head drops back to rest on Ric's shoulder and my glance wanders to the doorway. Max doesn't hide the sadness from his eyes before he turns away to head for the stairs. I hear the front door close and the sound of his Harley starting up.

I don't want him to be sad. I don't want him to leave now. I need my last memories of him to be happy.

Don't you DARE give up, Ethan! I refuse to lose you again. If you won't fight for yourself and your mate, I'll just have to fight enough for all of us.

The sound of gravel hitting the house has all of us tensing up. Daddy and Shaun have no clue what Max just sent me. I don't think I was supposed to hear it. Max knows what tomorrow means.

I don't want him to be angry...

Mr. Whiskers is suddenly in my arms and my thumb is in my mouth and Daddy is rocking me in our chair. I can't keep losing time like this on my last day.

"Don't cry my little bluebird," Daddy whispers as he rubs his hand in circles on my back.

When did I start crying?

Ric

Ethan finally drifted off to sleep after about an hour of alternating between sobs and panic attacks. I still have no clue what set him off this afternoon, but somehow Shaun asking about plans for the birthday party tomorrow triggered this episode. Maybe it's the stress of him not allowing himself time to really regress?

I've had my boy home for two and a half months now and he hasn't done a full regression at all. I never really thought anything of it because he still talks to his stuffies and spends his free time in his playroom. It's not like he's ignoring any responsibilities or anything. He finished all of his classes a couple weeks ago...

Ethan hasn't left the house once since his last final... That realization makes me pause at the door to my office...

My boy, who loves running around outside and talking to people, hasn't set foot out of the house for weeks...

I mean, yes, I have been a bit over the top with not allowing him to go downstairs by himself or cook anything. But have I been projecting my fears onto him? Have I overdone it and made him afraid to be around other people?

Before I go into my office to do some work, I shoot off a couple of texts. First to Dr. Rawlings to set up a therapy session as soon as possible. I need some tools and some professional advice to fix my shit before I mess up again with my mate. The second text is to Max. I don't know what is going on with him the last six months, but it needs to stop. It's affecting my boy and I won't have that.

> **Me:**
> My office. One hour.

The only reason I'm giving him an hour is because there's a good chance he is still on his bike and will need time to get back.

> **Head Warrior:**
> I've got shit to work out. Is this really
> necessary?

I stare at the message in a bit of shock. Since when does he think it's appropriate to question an order from his Alpha. He may be one of my best friends, but the only person who gets to question me as Alpha is my mate...

Challenge must be accepted and fought, my wolf pipes up.

Challenge? What challenge? He's just being a moody bastard.

> **Me:**
> One hour. That's an order.

I receive a thumbs up as a reply this time. Seeing his acknowledgement and acceptance of the order allows something inside me to uncoil a bit. I don't really understand why his questioning me makes me so tense all of a sudden.

He is the same, my wolf says cryptically.

Gee thanks, asshole. My wolf has been more and more secretive, and I can't decide if he's messing with me or if he's preparing me for something. Either way, I'm not getting more out of him tonight, so I turn my attention to the financial statements in front of me while I wait for Max to get back.

THREE

Ric

By the time I hear the garage opening, I'm almost finished making sense of the mess Connor made of everything by disappearing for the last two months or so. His whole mate thing coming right after the most expensive Christmas ever really didn't help us out at all. Leaving the financial stuff in my hands long term is a recipe for disaster. I finally give up after a while and put the papers away. Seems like it was just in time as my door swings open and Max comes in.

He looks like shit.

To be honest, he's looked horrible since we got back from Atlanta. He's been spending less and less time here and doesn't hang out with any of us. Even Seb and Bast have asked me what is up with him. I thought he'd at least be communicating with his warriors, but their questioning makes me think it's time for an intervention of sorts.

As he takes a seat in one of the chairs in front of my desk, I decide to just throw it out there and say fuck it.

"What the fuck is your problem lately?"

The way his head shoots up and his wolf growls before he can school himself is surprising. Since when does his wolf think it can show anger to his Alpha for a simple question?

I witness him rebuilding the walls in his mind. His posture straightens and his eyes lose the edge of anger. Yeah, this is gonna be fixed today or I'm sending him to Bennet. Something changed with his wolf while he was there with Ethan, and it altered everything between our wolves.

"Talk to me, Max. You're at the end of the rope here," I say softer. "Your men see that something is up. I can see it. And today you upset Ethan with your theatrics. If you're not up for the job, tell me. If you want to leave, tell me. Just don't be starting drama and shit in my pack for no reason."

I watch Max take a couple deep breaths before his shoulders sag. He seems to deflate and fold in on himself. With his head in his hands, he starts talking.

"I can't keep doing it, Bossman. It hurts to see him so scared and knowing he won't say anything."

I sit up straighter and know my eyes are likely as big as fucking saucers at his words. This is all about whatever is going on with Ethan. Max has seen this in my boy for months and never said a word to me, or anyone else for that matter.

I forcefully hold back the growl my wolf wants to vocalize. He doesn't understand that Max isn't a threat to our relationship with Ethan. Number one, he's one of my best friends. He'd never do that to me. More important is number two; Blue has never had eyes for anyone else. I've seen it in his memories and heard it in his every thought before Shaun put up that wall.

"I'm sorry, Ric," Max whispers as he lifts his gaze to meet my eyes. "I didn't know he was your mate when I started to love him."

WHAT. THE. FUCK?!

There is no holding back the growl as I shoot to my feet and almost leap across the desk to beat the shit out of him. Only the fact that he remains perfectly still, head tilted in submission, keeps me in control enough to stop and wait to hear the rest. It takes more effort than I'm comfortable with to control my wolf, but eventually I manage to signal for Max to continue. This had better be important.

"I've been looking for the last three and a half months for a way to break a fated bond."

I had just gotten my wolf settled, and I'm fighting the shift again. I'm not sure where Max is going with this, but he better clear it up quickly. My wolf is not happy with him at all...

"Not for you guys!" he exclaims as he takes in the change in my eyes. At least this admission placates the beast inside of me for the moment and I manage to wrestle myself back into my chair. For someone who I consider my brother, he's dangerously close to dying by my hands today...

"The night we picked little dude up at the warehouse, I met my fated mate," Max whispers almost to softly for me to hear it.

"That's a good thing, right?" I ask. I mean, fated mates are supposed to be gifts, blessings, perfect for us... so why is he looking to break a bond?

"He's not one of us, not a wolf," he says making sure to catch my eyes. "He's a vampire."

Realization hits with me as I know who he's talking about. There were only two vampires that Max could have scented enough to recognize as his and it certainly was not Edward.

"Ethan's cousin? Joshua?" I prompt him. He nods and I can hear the hitch in his voice as he continues to explain.

"The reason I was not here when Ethan took off that morning was because I met up with Josh, Sully, whatever he goes by... We met up after I dropped you guys off here.

"I've never seen someone so excited to meet with me. He was overjoyed that he didn't have to wait hundreds of years like his uncles or even decades like his father..." Max's pause lets me know the night wasn't all happy.

"Until he read my thoughts...

"My mind was on little dude," he argues his point to me. "In my defense, I've always had my mind as my safe place to say what I couldn't say out loud. I could love who I wanted there even though I had already resigned myself to the fact that I will never be with him... and my mate managed to see it all..."

The implications of what Max is telling me just keep piling up. Joshua Sullivan is the heir to the Eastern US Vampire Kingdom. His father rules the Western US and another uncle is in charge of the Central US from the Mississippi to the Rockies. My head warrior has essentially signed his death warrant by loving another, regardless of the fact that the one he loves is mine.

I guess the horror shows on my face because Max is quick to shake his head and explain, "He hasn't told anyone that his blood sang for me. No one knows we felt the sparks. And since vampires don't have omegas, there won't be a pregnancy. We just need to break the bond and no one will ever need to know."

He puts his head back in his hands and I can hear the strain in his voice, like he's choking back tears, "It's what we agreed. "

"That doesn't make it better!" I yell at him getting to my feet. I crouch in front of him and try to get through to him. "Fate has given you to each other and you're throwing it away because he saw in your mind that you loved his cousin before you even knew he existed?"

"Love... present tense," Max says with steel in his voice, his eyes daring me to question him. "I'm tired of hiding it. I've loved him since the first time I saw him. I've wanted to... no NEEDED to be his shield, his protector, his safety. Jackie being born is the only reason I didn't end my life when we lost Ethan nine years ago. I couldn't let another innocent suffer at the hands of your father...

"After Dick died, I was going to leave since the threat was gone, but by then the little shit had a grip on my heart," I can see the ghost of a smile flit briefly through his eyes before his features harden again.

"I resolved to stay until Jack gets his wolf... So that he can protect himself at least.

"Years passed and you gave me the head warrior position after your parents died. You trusted me, not only with a few, but with the whole pack. My heart had mended a lot thanks to that and the little sunshine.

"So when we got Ethan back, the old feelings didn't hit right away. I felt a tickle of them, but by the time I saw him again, you already knew he was your mate and I was able to convince myself and my wolf that he was at least safe enough with you.

"His plan for you with his heat broke the last of my hope, so I wanted to be the best friend I could be to the both of you... And it worked... mostly."

He pushes himself out of the chair and heads for the corner of the room. The walk to the table with the whiskey is a short one, but Max uses it to regroup his thoughts. This is the man I thought was unflappable. This is the man I always figured didn't feel things deeply.

Just how much have I hurt my friend over the years in my ignorance? How much of my friend is truly the man in front of me?

After knocking back two glasses, he turns to me to continue his explanation. I settle into one of the chairs to listen. I owe him this much at least.

"The holidays made me fall deeper for him. I mean, no one else ever understood me and was willing to break the law to get me gifts I would love..."

We both have a bit of a chuckle at that. I'm still fighting to get us off some of the government watchlists for my boy's purchases for gifts...

"And your kiss with him on New Year's after letting our wolves play made me jealous as all hell. It felt like my heart was breaking, but I still knew there was no hope for me. It didn't stop the feelings from existing, though. I had just resigned myself to an unrequited thing as long as little dude was happy.

"After Josh saw how I felt, he ran off." He pours another glass of my good whiskey and smirks at the amber liquid in front of him. "He's faster than even Ethan is when he's pissed..."

"Anyways, it took me a while to come to terms with the whole mate thing. My plan was to see you and Ethan together once more in order to give up on my feelings once and for all. Then, I was going to go beg my mate to give me a chance to get over my feelings. But you went and fucked everything up."

He chuckles the last part and collapses onto the couch under the window. "He ran from you. And then I spent almost an entire month in that house with him with no interference from you or my mate or *anyone* who could remind me why it was a bad idea to open my heart back up.

"I reinforced my mental walls knowing that Edward was there, so no one could read my thoughts. But I neglected to build walls around my heart. I fell more and more in love yet again while I deluded myself into believing he was done with you..."

The self-deprecation is dripping from his voice and it hurts me to see my friend, practically my brother, being in pain like this. It's weird that him wanting my mate is causing the pain, but I still don't like seeing him in pain...

"I redoubled my efforts to find a way to break the bonds of fate so I could free us both, convinced we would be happy together."

I can't hold back the derisive snort at that last comment. Max responds with a smirk before resuming his staring contest with the sky outside the window.

Yeah, I had fucked up royally then. But there's no way my Blue would have moved on with anyone short of me being dead. I've seen into his mind and Max is on the same level as Connor to Ethan. He's nothing more than a big brother figure.

"Josh and I met up again on the way to Shaun's cabin. He was supposed to be there with us to help guard Ethan against the fae. I guess I was a bit lax in my shielding because he saw that my love had grown over the last month or so, and he ran off before I could even explain. He wasn't even around long enough for Jack to notice he was there at all...just long enough to see the worst possible thing he could.

"Then, after chasing down the fae and everything, Ethan ran straight to you at that dirty ass motel in Georgia. He saw me over the railing and his face fell."

I watch as tears start to slide down to the cushion beneath his head.

"His face fucking fell when he saw me... Then, he saw you and he was alive in a way I hadn't seen since Christmas. That was the moment I knew I lost everything. I lost my mate, my best friend, and the love of my life in one instant..."

Scrubbing at his face quickly, he sits up and takes a moment to compose himself.

"I'll leave if you think that's best. I just need to make sure the babies are ok, same as I did with Jackie. Ethan said something to me that makes me really worried about him and the twins."

I get up and pour myself a drink and carry another over to Max on the couch. I sit down and prompt him with a nod to continue when I hand over his drink.

"He said something about me needing to be around to protect them from the start," Max utters throwing his head back to rest on the cushion behind him. "It was mostly mumbles, but I think he's worried that someone, or even he, will hurt the babes like he was hurt. He's terrified of something happening to them...and him not being able to stop it."

Ethan

Yet again I'm staring at the ceiling in our room. I woke up shortly after Ric left the room, but I don't want to be a bother. My birthday is in less than six hours... I'm pretty sure I'm going to die tomorrow.

Daddy thinks I don't know, but I heard it. I heard about the fact that the vampire in me is making me human for the babies. I have to die for them to live apparently, just like my mother and grandmother. I'm not dumb. I can put two and two together. And since tomorrow is their death anniversaries, I'm pretty sure fate will take me as well.

As much as I want to tell Daddy and let him hold me and protect me and make it all better, I can't put this on him. What I *can* do is get my big brother back here for his best friend. They're going to need each other more than ever.

I know the office door is closed while Ric is working, so I pick up the phone and send a text to Connor.

> **Me, Myself, and • •**
> Can you come over tomorrow? I want to see my big brother on my birthday.

He usually is quick to respond and I see the three dots appear and disappear a bunch of times before I finally get a response.

> **ConMan**
> Sorry, buddy. I have to miss your birthday, but I'll come visit soon.

No. No. No. No. No. No. No. No.

I can feel the panic rising in me. Mr. Whiskers is already crushed to my chest to the point that I can feel Stabby's handle digging into my sternum. I feel the bruise forming, but I just clutch him tighter. I didn't get to say goodbye last time. I need to say goodbye to my big brother. I can't hurt him like that again.

The door flies open and Daddy and Max rush into the room. Daddy is holding me almost as tight as I'm holding Mr. Whiskers. Why does it feel like my throat is on fire?

Daddy, please make it better. I don't want my last hours with you to be like this.

"It's ok, baby," he is saying straight into my ear, over and over. Why isn't he whispering? My throat hurts so much. I'm even tasting blood.

Is this how I die? It's too soon. I'm supposed to have a few more hours at least.

I don't want to die yet. I'm not ready.

"You're not going to die!" Max growls at me and my breath hitches with the shock of it. Max never growls at me. He gets growly *around* me but never with me, not for real... and now my throat isn't as burny anymore. I wonder why.

Daddy keeps rocking me gently and running his fingers through my hair. Now that the tears have started, I'm having trouble stopping them. I'm really going to miss getting held like this...

"Sweetheart, why were you screaming?"

I was screaming?

So that's why my throat went all itchy and burny and started bleeding... How could I be screaming and didn't know it? I wish I could ask my mother what the first signs were when she started to die with me. Maybe it's insanity?

"Ethan, baby, you need to focus and answer us, please," Daddy shakes my shoulders gently to bring my focus back to him and Max. "What set off the panic attack? Was it a dream? A memory?"

Oh, right. That was a panic attack. I'm not dying yet. I have until tomorrow still. That's a relief. Releasing a big breath, I hand my phone to Daddy to show him the text with Connie. He starts growling and passes my phone to Max, who is still growling softly. Neither one of them looks happy right now. That isn't right.

I need my last day to be happy and fun, like Christmas was. That can't be the last time we all were happy together. I hadn't found my bestest friend again yet. I didn't know my dad or Grandpa Eddie yet. Celeste hadn't found me. All of my people are here now and I need all of them to be happy... even when I'm not here anymore.

Max punches a hole right through the door... I can't help the hiccupping giggle that escapes at the thought that we should just not have a door on this room if we keep breaking them...

Not we... Ric. He doesn't need a door anyways. He'll need to be able to go to the babies quicker anyways...

Daddy says something to Max and then lays me down and tucks me in. Not Daddy... Ric. I don't need to worry about what they're saying. I just need them to be happy again...

I don't want to sleep yet, but that panic attack really did take a lot out of me. I'll just rest my eyes a bit and get a full day tomorrow, as much as I can.

I can feel some shifting next to me on the bed, but I don't bother to open my eyes. I know I'm safe enough at least until tomorrow. I just have to figure out how to get everyone here to have a good day before I have to say goodbye... I don't wanna go...

Ric

I'm going to kill my Beta. Thank the gods that Jackie is at his friend's house for dinner tonight because Connor managed to upset Ethan enough to completely shatter the wall Shaun put up in his mind. My phone is blowing up from every pack member in a five mile radius asking if my mate is alright.

I swear my heart stopped when I heard his screams in my head. Max beat me to the office door and as soon as the seal was broken, the sound of anguish echoing through the house was deafening. I started leaving the door cracked when Ethan is just napping so that I wouldn't have to keep replacing the door when his nightmares hit. So the door getting slammed open only put a small hole in the wall. Then, Max put a hole in the door with his fist at what we found out...

I can't blame him though. It took almost twenty minutes to get Ethan to stop screaming. He was still trying to scream long after his vocal chords gave up. I couldn't fight my own sobs as I heard all of his thoughts and his pain. Knowing he was screaming, but not being able to reach him to get him to stop was probably the most useless I've ever felt.

I'm lucky Max was there, even if I do have to buy another bedroom door. I left him to watch over Ethan and maybe figure out this whole "tomorrow is the last day" and "need to say goodbye" shit that he's got spinning around up there. My boy talks to Max about the darker stuff before he'll open up to me. I'm not jealous over it, much...

I just wish we could get over his fear of doctors so we can both work on our stuff to be a better couple. Therapy is already helping me to understand how to realize that some things are just outside of my control. It's helping me to be a better Alpha, a better brother, and a better mate. I don't think Ethan is broken, but I hate to see him struggling and questioning things because he doesn't want to burden us.

Maybe I can convince him that way... letting him burden a stranger so he doesn't worry us...

I spend the whole run over to Connor's house thinking these things so that I can keep my wolf inside of me. I'm sure Connor realizes what he did by sending that text. He's within the radius... But he didn't check in. That worries me more than anything else.

I stop at the edge of his driveway to slow my breathing and make sure I have a handle on my wolf. Between the conversation with Max and now Connor pulling this shit... it's amazing my wolf hasn't just gone feral and killed them both and let Seb and Bast take over their positions...

Not a bad idea, my wolf sends to me on a snarl.

I'm starting to agree with him.

I notice there are no lights on in the house. I know Connor is home. As the Alpha, I can locate any member of the pack if I focus. I usually don't try, but the fact that Connor knows I'm out here but he's still trying to hide is pissing me off again.

My phone vibrating in my pocket breaks my gaze away from the front of the house. Pulling it out, I see it's the hospital calling...

Last thing I need right now is for something to have happened to Jackie and I gotta go into town. The kids were going to see a movie in town with their teacher after dinner. Mr. Morrison is supposed to be treating a bunch of the boys from the class since his nephew is visiting from California. I slipped Zach some money for it since I know teachers don't make enough to splurge for theater money for seven boys.

Before it rings out to voicemail, I swipe up, fully prepared to abandon my questioning of my Beta, even though it won't make things any better for him in the long run... "This is Alaric Jameson."

"Ric? It's Shaun. Is Ethan alright?"

This is not the call I was expecting and a wave of relief sweeps through my body to the point my wolf even stands down. Then, I realize...

The hospital is over forty miles away. How far did the psychic screaming reach?

"He's getting there, but your wall is gone," I tell him, turning back to the house in time to see the curtain in the living room flutter. "He got a text and it sent him into the mother of all panic attacks."

"Ok good," he exhales before stammering, "I mean, not good as in he had a panic attack, but good that it was just the wall crashing under force. I felt it break and was worried with what tomorrow is and and and he's been so stressed and trying to hide it and..."

"Breathe, Shaun. What's this about tomorrow? It's just his birthday."

The pause on the other end of the line makes me take notice that there's something obvious that I'm definitely missing here.

"Um Alpha..."

Shaun stops and starts a few times before finally coming out and saying it. "Ethan's birthday is also the anniversary of both his mother's and grandmother's death. Both died in childbirth. And he's pregnant... Early labor is not only possible, but expected for both omegas and multiples..."

Oh. Fuck. Me... It never even crossed my mind.

"I take it from your silence, you hadn't even considered it, right?"

I grunt an affirmation while my mind is spinning out, replaying all of the events and conversations over the last two months. I'm realizing just how withdrawn my boy has become... how insistent he is that we all need to be happy and ready for the babies even though we all assure him there's plenty of time...

"He asked me yesterday if the babies would be able to live if something happened to him at this point in the pregnancy. I didn't put it together until just now with the wall crashing," Shaun says bringing me back to the conversation. "Ric, I truly believe he thinks he's going to die tomorrow like his mother and grandmother. I just didn't realize it until I thought something actually happened with the wall coming down."

"He's not dying tomorrow. He's not dying in childbirth. My boy is going to be around to raise these kids with all the love and support that he never got for himself," I growl into the phone as my wolf is struggling to find a way to protect our mate. Only, there's no real threat to him but his own fear...

"What set him off? Who sent the text?" Shaun asks bringing me back to the fact that I'm still on the phone instead of beating the shit out of a big brother who should fucking know better. I look to the darkened house before replying.

"We'll talk more in depth later, Shaun. I have to kick someone's ass."

"So it WAS him," he mutters before I disconnect the call. I don't need to add any more fuel to the fire between these two. They need to either fully reject each other or fuck each other and complete the bond. This in-between bullshit needs to end.

At the door, I raise my fist to pound, but it opens before I even make contact. The is the first time I'm seeing Connor in over a month and he looks worse that Max. What the fuck is wrong with my men and them not doing what they should to claim their mates? They are all fucking miserable and now they're affecting my relationship!

"Whatever the fuck your problem is with your mate, fix it!" I snarl at him pushing my way into the house. "You are GOING to see your brother tomorrow and you are GOING to be happy and not look like a homeless drug addict. Consider it an order from your Alpha."

I can see him struggling to refuse, but in the end, Connor just hangs his head and shuffles into the living room. He manages to flop down on the couch, but how he knows it's there is beyond me. There's so much trash and takeout and laundry strewn about that I can't say for sure where the furniture is and where it's just piles of junk...

"What the fuck happened to you, dude?" I sigh because I can't stay angry when he's this pathetic.

He throws his forearm over his eyes to block the little bit of moonlight that is filtering into the room through the curtains. "Is Ethan alright? I know I hurt him, but I honestly didn't think it would hit him like that."

He chokes out a sound that could only be described as pure despair. "I can't stop hurting him, can I?"

I don't think he meant for me to hear that part.

Do I play the Alpha card and force a confrontation? Do I play the best friend card and commiserate to lift him up even though he's being a dumbass? Do I play the brother's boyfriend card and beat the shit out of him?

Okay, the last one is purely selfish and I'm only half joking with it. Some stress relief right about now wouldn't be unwelcome...

"If I promise to be there tomorrow, just for a bit, will you let it go for now?" he asks me while I am still picturing using him as a human punching bag.

Taking a deep breath, I nod an affirmative to his question. My Beta gets a reprieve for now. He knows he fucked up. He knows he needs to shape up and get his shit together... not for himself, but for Ethan. I know there's nothing in this world that matters more to him than his little brother...

As soon as I'm outside, I hear the snick of the deadbolt being turned on the door. The old me would insist on being the one to fix this, fix him. Doc Rawlings has helped me realize I need to let go sometimes. Connor is a grown man. I've said my piece. Now, it's up to him.

FIVE

Ethan

Somehow, I managed to sleep through the night. The room is lit up with the mid-morning sunshine and I realize I've already missed some important and precious hours with my family. But that's alright... as long as they all come today and I can see them all one last time.

Enough of that one last time bullshit, Little Wolf.

GRANDPA EDDIE IS HERE!

I try to jump out of bed only to remember that my tummy makes it significantly more difficult to do any kind of jumping lately... so I make do with rolling and scooching myself to the edge to be able to get out of bed. Luckily, I am still kind of dressed from yesterday, so I don't have to worry about the whole bending over to put on pants struggle that I've started to have to deal with most days.

The babies love to play trampoline with my bladder when I put on pants... still not willing to try diapers though. Daddy says he's not getting rid of them until we're all done with the pregnancy just in case. I'm pretty sure I'm not changing my mind on that one.

Pushing my footsies into my grumpy raccoon slippers, I grab Mr. Whiskers and start the walk toward the stairs. It's getting more and more difficult to go down them the further along my pregnancy gets. I can't do the scooch without possibly hurting the babies. I'm afraid I'm going to fall down if I try to go down by myself...

I want to see my family, but I'm too scared to go down the steps... again. Why is it always the steps?

The first tears start blurring my vision and I wipe messily at my face. This is the last time they'll see me. I can't be crying over the steps. I have to be a big boy. I have to be happy today. I need them to remember me happy.

There's a woosh and suddenly Gramps is in front of me on the steps. I giggle at the slight breeze that follows almost a full second after he stops. It makes my hair tickle my ears...

Grandpa Eddie takes me by the arm and helps me down the stairs like he's escorting me to a fancy ball. The thought of it makes me giggle again seeing as how I'm in pajama pants and silly slippers. He leads me into the kitchen where everyone yells out "Surprise!" and a bunch of glitter rains down EVERYWHERE...

Daddy doesn't let me play with glitter cuz he says he doesn't need craft herpes infecting the whole house, but he's smiling with everyone else, so I guess it's ok for today. That's good though. Today needs to be a special day.

Suddenly everyone isn't so happy anymore. They all look a bit worried and sad. This isn't supposed to happen. Today is supposed to be happy memories... only happy memories. There's enough sadness coming...

"Ethan, sweetie?"

I turn to see Mama Lisa heading over to me. I miss Sunday

dinners with her and Dad. I know Mr. Whiskers misses them. Maybe Daddy can take him over there when I'm gone so he won't be lonely and he can go back to protecting Mama Lisa.

Someone let's out a noise that sounds sad and I try to look around, but Dad, not Daddy pulls me in tight for a hug before I can figure out who made the noise.

"Remember who you are, son," he whispers in my ear. "You are the firstborn. Nothing will happen to you."

But that's not true, though. I can still die. It just means I come back, but the babies would die. In order for them to live, I can't come back, right? That's what happened last time. That's why I have the scar. Dad is wrong. He doesn't know…. Right?

I feel myself being pushed into someone else's arms and I melt. This is Daddy. This is my mate. I can feel the satisfaction of my wolf at being embraced, not just because of panic, but because we're loved. I'm going to miss this… Will I miss it? Is there an afterlife? It's always just been a void for me, so I don't know if that's just a limbo place or if that's it. That would really suck if we just poof into the void and have to chill in the darkness all alone forever…

"Shaun, is there anything you can do to put the wall back up?" Daddy calls out from over my head.

Wait? The wall is down? I'm broadcasting again?

A bunch of nodding heads all around the kitchen cause all of the blood to rush simultaneously to my cheeks and out of the rest of my body. I feel like I'm going to throw up or pass out or something, but Daddy just holds me tighter while his wolf starts making this weird humming noise, almost like a purring sound… I didn't know our wolves could do that.

Only mates comes the gravelly voice of Ric's wolf. I still find it really nifty that his wolf figured out how to speak to me using my mind speak thingy.

"Shaun?" Daddy asks again with a chuckle.

"Almost done," I hear from across the room before I feel a click inside my head. Now that the wall is back up, I understand just how open I actually was without it.

"When did it go down?" I ask my bestie as he joins me at the island where Daddy set me on my stool.

"Last night, little one," Daddy says. "When you were screaming, the wall shattered."

I feel my cheeks heating up again and I sheepishly hung my head... "Sorry..."

"You don't have to apologize for someone else's behavior!" Shaun growls out while glaring across the room. I follow his line of sight to see my big brother.

He came after all... I'm so happy!

Ric

Well I was hoping to give my boy his perfect birthday with all of his family before everyone found out what he is so afraid of, but of course the wall being down made that a moot point. I think most of Ethan's thoughts still went over Jackie's head so we should be safe to resume the party now that Shaun put the wall back up.

Leaving the two boys to talk at the island, I scan the crowd to make sure everyone who is important to my bluebird is here. Jackie is in the living room with his friend now that the surprise is over. Max is hovering next to the fridge, trying not to stare at my boy. Josh is by his uncle, trying not to stare at my warrior. Seb and Bast are... well Seb is coming in from the basement followed by Celeste. Bastian was just here, I could have sworn... Celeste's brother follows her but he looks crushed as he starts making his way to the birthday boy.

Looking back at Ethan, I see his shy pose transform into one of pure joy. I follow his gaze and I see Connor standing in the doorway. Good... the asshole needs to be here. He still looks like shit but it's miles better than yesterday.

Turning back to my boy, I can tell he's itching to go over to his brother, but needs help getting off the stool. We really do need to work on his fears, but today is going to be all fun.

Shaun and the fae boy... why can't I remember his name?... they help Ethan off the stool, but before he can make his way to Connor, the fae gives him a hug and whispers in his ear. When they pull apart, Ethan looks confused and a bit sad, but the fae boy is barely holding himself together. At my boys nod, he takes off, not quite running out of the house, but definitely making a hasty exit.

"What's all that about, Blue?" I ask him as I come up from behind.

"Felix just found out he has a mate, Daddy," he whispers as he buries his face into my chest. "Why don't the fae get mates like we do? Why is it all messed up for them? It's not fair!"

I look up to see Shaun speaking to Celeste by the door before he runs out in the same direction Felix went. At least I know the kid's name now. But back to the question my boy is asking... Everything I've ever learned about the fae is that their unions are almost entirely political. Occasionally there will be a love match, but I've never heard of fated pairings in all the studies my father forced on me.

"The fates provide for the fae, just as they do the rest of us, Little Wolf," Edward says coming up to the island with a plate of cookies and a sippy cup of milk. He knows what his grandson needs right now and it's definitely not being a grown up... or at least not fully. "Most fae don't hear the bells of fate anymore because they've forgotten to listen."

"We haven't forgotten to listen, old man," Celeste mumbles as she snatches a cookie from the plate before Ethan even sees they're there. "The fates stopped ringing the bells for us a long time ago when the King rejected the match fate provided him in favor of the second Queen."

At my look she gives a slight nod and whispers, "Kestion the asswipe's mother."

The foul language brings a giggle from the area of my chest as my little bluebird resurfaces to join his party. There's a lot of chuckles at his awed whisper of "Cookies!" like they just magically appeared. Even Connor cracks a smile, but I'm pretty sure that only happened because Shaun left for the time being.

I'm Alpha, not a freaking relationship guru. These mates popping up all over the place need to find somewhere else to work their shit out...

The giggle in front of me makes me look to see a boy who

somehow managed to get chocolate in his hair from cookies that had no chocolate... Huh... The mysteries of the universe...

SIX

<u>Ethan</u>

This has been the bestest birthday I have ever had! It's sad that everyone is leaving the house now, but after my seventeen millionth yawn around my thumb, Daddy said it's time to call it a night. If I had to pick a perfect last day, today would have been it. My whole family, my found family both blood and chosen, they all showed up for me.

For. Me...

Not for some way to show off how important they are, but to actually celebrate my birthday just because they love me...

I'm loved... by more than just Daddy and Connor.

Fuck! Now my eyes are leaking again... Daddy looks a bit worried, but I smile and wave to let him know these are happy tears, just like the last fifty times today. He points to the hall to let me know he's going to walk the last of our guests out, so I nod and wave bye to Mama Lisa, Dad, and Sully. My cousin gives me a funny look but blows me a kiss before following Daddy to the door.

Everyone is gone now, except for Daddy. I don't want him to have to watch, but he won't leave me alone anymore. It's not fair! Why do I have to die when I finally know what it's like to be happy and loved and wanted? Why can't I live? Why don't I get to keep the love?

I sit on the couch and pull my knees up as much as I'm able to. Mr. Whiskers is laying across my belly. I wish I had two of him so that my babies will always be protected. Right now, he's doing his part. I really should have gotten them their own nightmare hunters before today. There was just so much to do that I forgot and now there's no more time...

My tears aren't happy anymore. I'm scared. There's only a few hours left in the day. There's not enough time. I'm not ready to say goodbye. The babies aren't big enough and Shaun isn't here. I hate the hospital, but I'm about to ask Daddy to take me there.

I need to be there for the babies to have a chance. That's what Shaun said. He said it's too early unless they could get them immediately into a special breathing thingy called a nickel or something.

"You sure these are still happy tears, Blue?"

I startle as Daddy's arm goes around my shoulders. I swear I try to stop the sobs, but my body doesn't listen and I collapse into Ric's side sounding more animalistic than my wolf ever has. I don't wanna go! I don't wanna leave him!

"Oh, Sweetheart," Ric breathes into my hair, pulling me fully into his lap. "You're not going anywhere today."

It takes me an embarrassingly high number of attempts to form words, but I finally manage to get it out. "But my mother and grandmother... this day... cursed..."

I get enough out that Daddy hugs me a little tighter. He waits until my tears slow down before speaking.

"You're not cursed to die today, baby. Your mother and grandmother both died because of injuries inflicted by Connor's grandfather, not because of a curse."

Ric

The day went so well that it completely slipped my mind that my boy believes he's going to die today. Holding him as tight as I can without crushing him or the babies, I keep repeating myself over and over, waiting for my words to sink in. His grandmother's mate, Connor's grandfather, was a downright nasty son of a bitch who beat his mate and kids, and even Connor, when he was drunk.

I don't know if our parents were ever aware of it, or even cared, but Elizabeth Welling took more than a few beatings to protect Connor when we were toddlers. I'm pretty sure he blocked it out, but it scared me enough to remember bits and flashes. Doc has been doing a lot of regression hypnosis with me to help me make sense of my survivor's guilt. I need to get over myself so that I can be here for my boy and my family.

"But... but... but..." Ethan is struggling to get his words out in between the gasping sobs. I want him to calm down, but we need to put this to bed before he falls asleep. "They both died today... And I don't want to leave you anymore, Daddy!"

He's breaking my heart here...

"I won't let you leave. I won't let death claim you, today or any other day." I grab his chin and gently force him to meet my eyes. "The Goddess herself couldn't stop me from keeping you right here by my side, alive and healthy and loved."

The despair in his eyes is flickering as I watch the hope start to take hold. Seeing him like this feels like someone is taking an ice dagger to my heart; I can only imagine how bad this would be if Shaun had not put the wall back up. It is taking every speck of my self-control not to take over and try to force Ethan to believe.

Fix mate, my wolf grumbles in my head.

Every instinct is pushing me to make it right. My wolf is

pushing me... But Ethan needs to do this himself. I need to just be support for him.

"King Edward shared with me his memory of the day you were born," I whisper when the tears finally slow again. "He also shared the memory he got from John Sinclair when he found your mother and took her to the hospital... AND the memories he took from the doctors and nurses that tried to save her life.

"She was beaten by her stepfather and left for dead while the bastard went to Dayton to get drunk. It was only chance that John happened to stopped by. According to the memory, he was going to ask your mother to watch Connor so that he and his mate could have a romantic date that night."

The scrunch of my Ethan's nose is adorable. No kid likes to think of their parents being intimate, but in his current mindset I'm sure his reaction is more exaggerated. My bluebird isn't quite all grown up, but he's not exactly fully regressing either.

He snuggles into me and mumbles something against my shoulder. I have to ask him to repeat it twice and eventually only the threat of a tickle attack gets him to say it.

"They didn't interact at all if there wasn't an audience," he whispers as if the very words are going to result in violence. "I can't even picture them on a date."

I don't discount his memories, but I also saw the memory direct from John's point of view. That man loved his mate, at least at that time. I'm not sure what happened to change things or if perhaps he just gave up trying to win her over, but now that Ethan's said it, I can't recall them ever looking at each other with affection.

"Well, the way I see it, we're already miles ahead of all of our parents in the romance department," I tell him with a little tug on his earlobe. His answering giggle is enough to let me know that he's starting to feel better.

"Do you want to watch a movie here or up in bed, my little Blue?"

He takes his time to consider and all I can think of is pulling his bottom lip away from his teeth. At least when he's little, it's his thumb. I worry he's going to end up splitting his lip one of these days from biting it in an attempt to stay grown up...

"I want the big screen, but I want to be comfy," he whines softly. "You choose, Daddy."

Without giving him a chance to brace himself, I lift him straight from my lap into a bridal carry and head for the stairs. I'm taking the giggling birthday boy to bed and showing off his new flat screen on the wall in our room. No more laptop or tablet for movies with cuddles...

Almost four hours and two superhero movies later, my boy is still fighting the exhaustion that has been pulling at him all day. When the clock hits midnight and a new day starts, I see the remaining tension flow right out of his body. Shortly after, his snores fill the room, so I turn off the television. Before I put my phone away for the night, I shoot off one last text message.

Me:
Thanks for being on call.

It takes less than ten seconds to get Shaun's reply, but that's a worry for the morning.

SEVEN

Ethan

It took almost a full six months since my heat before I started getting cravings. I can't decide if they started because I finally accepted that my birthday isn't cursed or if they started because the babies are big enough now to be demanding. Shaun says it's because my body needs certain nutrients, but I prefer to think my babies are just having competitions to see who is better at making Daddy turn green.

Pickles have become a staple with any dipping sauce — the spears though, not the chips. And none of that bread and butter crap. Even hormones can't make those things taste good.

Last night, we managed to send Daddy running for the bathroom when he walked into the kitchen to see me dipping a dill pickle spear into caramel syrup and then into those fried onion crispy thingies that people put on the green beans for the holidays.

It was AMAZEBALLS!

But Ric moved almost as fast as me to get out of the room when he saw it.

Oh, well. At least it shouldn't be too bad with the cookout today.

I always enjoyed the Fourth of July growing up because it meant I got a reprieve from everything. Fake Mom threw the pack barbecue every year and Fake Dad manned the grill. He would let me hang out by him and would give me the hot dogs that got too burnt for everyone else.

I think he secretly knew I liked them better burnt and did it on purpose. Fake Mom only let me have it because gods forbid she serve burnt food to her guests.

Waddling to the kitchen is easier now that Daddy has moved us down into the guest suite that Connie was using before. I'm still a bit freaked out at the idea of trying to navigate stairs, especially now that I can't see past my belly. I won't even walk a normal pace for fear of tripping and hurting the babies.

I waddle like a penguin everywhere in the house, only on the ground floor though. No steps. No outside.

I may not have died on my birthday, but there's still a good chance I'm going to give up the goat, or whatever the saying is, when I give birth. The only thing I'm focusing on right now is making sure these kids stay inside me as long as possible so that we don't have to go to the hospital.

I still have a hate/hate relationship with doctors, although I think if it's just Shaun and nurses, I might be able to handle it now.

"Blue? Guests are arriving! Do you need a hand?" Daddy's voice calls out from the patio doors. He and Max spent the last week turning our backyard into an oasis of fairy lights and comfy seating.

When I reach the door, I see that Ric laid out my slip-on shoes so that I don't have to worry about bending over to tie laces. That's really sweet of him and all, but my feet feel like water balloons, and I don't want to try and force them into anything confining.

The flip flops on the shoe rack would work, but I hate flip flops with a passion... or rather they hate me. I fall more often wearing those than I do when there's ice everywhere outside. And barefoot is completely out of the question. What if I step on something?

I'm not sure how long I have been standing here staring at the shoes before I notice Max coming from deeper inside the house. When did he come into the house?

"Try these for today, little dude," he tells me, handing me some hard soled slippers with little star poof-balls on the toesies. He even kneels down and helps me slip them onto my feet.

I smile at him, letting him truly see how grateful I am for his assistance. Ric has been running himself ragged this last month or so since my birthday, and I'm really happy that he has a good friend like Max to help him not burn out. My footsies aren't as important as running the pack, so I don't mind my buddy lending a hand at all if it means Daddy can do his job better.

Now, if we could only get my brother's head out of his ass long enough to get him back to work...

Ric wouldn't be anywhere near as run down if Connor would fucking man up and work his shit out with Shaun. I love them both, but the eight year old in the house is more mature than they are right now.

Speaking of Jack, I see him on the far side of the yard with some of the kids from his class. It really warms me on the inside knowing he has friends and that there's not really any bullying in our pack anymore. Any instances at the school and Zach is calling me up to formulate a plan. The kids get a talk, but the parents face actual punishment.

I'm making sure this shit is handled from the top down and if the parents don't like it, they're free to leave my damn pack.

Ric

It takes a while, but Ethan finally emerges from the house using his newly minted penguin walk. He's so adorable and beautiful, all round and growing our children; however, he believes he's a walking barn most days. I never understood what people meant when they said their love was beautiful when pregnant. I mean, who sees beauty in someone miserable, swollen, sweating, and farting all of the time? Apparently, I do because my boy is the most amazing sight to me right now.

"I like my new slippers, Daddy," he whispers to me when he manages to waddle over to the outdoor fireplace that I've just finished setting up. It's too warm out to start the fire while the sun is up, but I wanted to stack the wood and get it prepped so that we can light the fire at sundown.

Humming an agreement, I take a deep sniff of his hair, taking in his scent. Some days his scent is apple pie a la mode with chocolate ice cream. Other times it's closer to a mulled cider, heavy with cloves and spices. But every day, I smell the sweet scent of ripe apples and I'm reminded of home and safety. It's the smell of my mother's kitchen. It's the scent of love.

I love the way his scent has changed with the pregnancy. It's deeper, sweeter somehow... and it's distracting as much as it's calming.

What did he say? New slippers?

I hear a snort from the grill area and look over to see Max trying to hide a laugh in a coughing fit. So at least now I know where my boy got new slippers. Glancing down at his feet, I can admit they are cute... and appropriate for the day. The red and white striped slippers with the blue pom poms really fit the holiday motif so Ethan doesn't have to worry about being judged for wearing slippers outside.

I hate that Max thinks of these things before me. My wolf still is not happy about the fact that another man is in love with our mate, but I've accepted that any help is welcome at this point.

Shaun says the next month or so is critical to keep him calm as possible to lessen the prematurity of the babies. According to him, they are coming early no matter what... We just don't know how early. All he knows is that if the babies don't start to come naturally by the middle of August, he's going to want to induce.

The thought terrifies me, but at the same time I would rather us be safe ahead of time rather than panicked and risking everyone's lives by prolonging it all...

I feel the movement against my hip from the babies. That's my signal that we need to sit Papa down and start feeding him foods that aren't going to make me want to hurl. As much as he is in love with pickles right now, I've made sure that none have come out to the backyard for today's cookout.

The next few hours go by without incident and the whole pack seems to have enjoyed themselves greatly. My boy is leaning against Shaun, half asleep, but he refuses to go inside until after the fireworks show. His sleepy giggles flow across the yard while the younger kids are chasing fireflies at the trees' edge.

As I go to sit on the other side of Shaun, Ethan reaches up for me to pick him up like a little toddler would reach for their parent. Everyone at the firepit laughs at him, but he doesn't care. I gently lift him from the lounger and keep him on my lap as I take my seat. Max lights the wood that I set up earlier in the day and offers to grab more drinks while we sit and wait for the techies to start the show.

Ethan is going in and out of sleep, but I'm not going to force him to stay awake right now. I'll wake him up when the show starts. For now, he's growing people inside of him. He needs rest. It has been a long day, and his first one outside in over two months.

"Have you convinced him to come in for an exam yet?" Shaun asks me, popping the cap off a fresh beer from Max. "I can only do so much with my witchcraft and Celeste has exhausted her sight on him already."

The soft snores coming from the boy in my lap means he is too deeply asleep to be listening, which is a good thing. We all agree that we need to prevent panic attacks as much as possible right now, and a quick and easy way to trip over one is to mention doctors or hospitals. But I agree with Shaun. We need to get him checked out with more than just magic. There's frankly not enough literature out there on omega pregnancies, especially with multiples.

Seb and Bastian join us around the fire, the latter looking like he's swallowed something foul. "Our Ma says omega or not, twins are painful enough to swear off sex forever. Guess that's why we never got any younger siblings," Seb breathes out, reaching for the cooler that has the sodas inside. Bast smacks him upside the head knocking him to the ground, making us all laugh.

The noise wakes Ethan up, but before any of us can feel bad about it, music starts blasting from the speakers around the yard. All of my attention goes to the boy in my lap and the wonder on his face as the sky lights up to the sounds of classic rock and explosives.

EIGHT

<u>Ethan</u>

"I can't believe I let you talk me into this!"

This back-stabbing, no good, double crossing piece of shit were-witch that I used to call my best friend has just parked his ancient monstrosity of a car in the hospital parking lot — with me in the passenger seat.

Stupid logic and guilt and puppy eyes from Jackie and suddenly I want to push my limits and go inside that building again.

"Nope..." I can feel the panic rising. I can't do this. I can't go inside.

Last time I was here, the fae wanted to kidnap me. The time before that, a doctor scared the shit out of me and didn't even care. Before that was when I first came out of the lab and was still in survival mode.

Well... actually I suppose I was here when I was dead after that gathering thingy, but I wasn't alive for that so I don't count it.

There's a weird high pitched whining noise coming from the car. I know Shaun is fixing this up so he can recreate Baby from Supernatural, but maybe he should get a professional to look at it. If he ever gets his head out of his ass with Connie, he'd look at it. My big brother has always been great with cars and bikes and really anything with moving parts.

Shaun knocks on the window next to me. He is at my door waiting for me to unlock it...

When the fuck did he get out of the car?

The car is off? That means the whining noise is... me...

I need Daddy for this...

"Your Daddy is already here," Shaun says through the window. "He just parked his SUV and is walking over. Now, unlock the door so that I can yank you upright and fix your wall again."

"You alright, baby?" Ric asks, clearing the back end of the Impala while I do my little rocking dance to stand up from the open doorway. I refuse to let Shaun help me up right now. I'm mad at him for making me do this and my wolf's growl echoes across the mostly empty parking lot.

Shaun chuckles as he closes the door on his clunker and directs us to the main hospital entrance opposite the emergency room. Just turning that direction helps to calm me a little bit. At least I'm not likely to run into the meanie doctor again since he was in the emergency room...

I never disliked pink before today, but we are bombarded by pink and baby blue and just baby stuff EVERYWHERE getting off the elevator on the ninth floor. This can't be typical decoration for a baby doc in a hospital, right?

"It looks like Godzilla ate a baby shower and then threw up in the lobby."

I slap my hand over my mouth on a gasp. I did not mean to say that out loud!

Luckily, the nurses waiting for us laughed. Shaun and Daddy just shake their heads at me. I guess stopping the leak from my brain wasn't enough to stop the leaking from my mouth... Filter is officially gone thanks to my stress today, but at least no more signs of panic so far.

The nurses bring me and Ric back to one of the exam rooms while Shaun says he's going to get the machines we need. I'm already nervous, but as long as Daddy doesn't leave me alone for even a second, I think I can get through this...

I'm pretty sure I checked out mentally for a bit because the next thing I know, my feet are in stirrups and Shaun is between my legs getting up close and personal with my asshole. Before I can even build up to a freak out, Ric kisses the back of my hand that he's holding. It's not much but it's enough to ground me into the present.

"Looks good down here, Buddy. Let's get some pictures and we can get you out of here before the place starts to fill up for the morning."

Why the hell would he need pictures of my asshole?

I hear the stool rolling across the floor, but I'm not looking at anything but the ceiling. There's a silly poster of a kitten hanging from a tree branch tacked onto the ceiling right above me. The drastic difference between what I remember of exams and what I'm experiencing is making it easier to stay relatively calm right now. It is imperative that Daddy doesn't let go of me, though.

My mind wanders for a bit, flashing back to my birthday while I wait for Shaun to take his damn pictures so we can leave already...

Everyone is here! Well, almost everyone. Felix ran off because he got scared that Bastien is going to not want him when his sister is around... Something about fae twins sharing everything. If you ask me, Bast hasn't even glanced at Celeste except in confusion. Shaun took off after Felix to try and talk to him. He said it was to be helpful, but I know he's running away from Connor.

Then there's Sully constantly on the sidelines unless Max leaves the area... Today is the first time I've gotten to see everyone I love and care about in the same day and they all came for me... I'm loved...

"Don't cry, little bluebird," Daddy says as he wipes the tears from my eyes.

"Happy tears, Daddy. Happy tears," I mumble while the room starts singing the Happy Birthday song to me.

"Ready to get the first photos of the future models?" a nurse asks as she lifts up my shirt to uncover my ginormous belly. The jolt back to the present makes me jump, but I play it off well enough. I think they think I'm just not good with touch. They can believe that if they want.

And now I realize the pictures they wanted were those ultrasound thingies. That makes more sense. Stress brain means dumbass Ethan apparently...

The gel stuff Shaun squirts on my baby bump is cold as fuck and I let out a string of cussing that makes one nurse blush and the other snort. The snorting nurse looks familiar now that I'm looking at her a bit more... I can't shake the feeling I know her...

"How do I know you?" I didn't mean to say that out loud either, but she ducks her head and chuckles.

"Remember your Christmas shopping accident?" she asks me with a smirk.

That's where I know her from! She was my nurse in the Emergency Room that sent the meanie doctor flying into the wall. She's part of Dad's pack...

"Daddy, can we invite her to the next cookout?" I ask turning to Ric while Shaun is using this game controller looking thing to press into my belly. "She sent the meanie doc flying last time. I like her!"

Ric just chuckles and tells her she's more than welcome to visit our pack and our house whenever she wants, to which she gives a full belly laugh and agrees to come, especially after the babies are here.

Speaking of the babies, my bestie is looking more serious than I am comfortable with while he keeps moving that thing around on my bump. I can feel the twins pushing and kicking at it, and my bladder, so he better hurry this up.

"E-man... Ric... I don't know how to tell you this," he starts and my heartrate starts to rise. There's something wrong with the babies. By me living, they're going to die. I killed my babies... I knew I shouldn't be a papa...

"Easy there, Blue. Let him finish," Ric chides gently. I take a few deep breaths to try and relax, then nod for Shaun to continue.

"Early on, both my magic and Celeste's recognized you were having twins."

Ric and I both nod. This is an established fact. Wait...

DID I LOSE ONE OF THE BABIES?!?! Did the bitch take one after all????

Everyone in the room grabs their heads while I'm trying to calm my breathing. I don't know what's wrong with them, but I'm gonna be going to fuck up a Goddess in a minute here as soon as I can make sure I'm not going to put my remaining baby in danger...

"Shit, man! Chill!" Shaun shouts at me. "Quit blasting my walls to fucking splinters!"

Ric

I haven't had a headache like this since the night Ethan was taken and I was fighting the hangover the next morning. Ethan's psychic blast not only shattered the wall Shaun put up, but it also knocked down every supe in likely a ten mile radius at least. One of the nurses passed out, the human one. Apparently, she's dated a vampire, so she's one of the ones on call to assist with supernatural pregnancies.

It's immediate relief when Shaun is able to construct a new barrier in Ethan's mind. The pain takes a minute or two to recede enough for me to realize what the blast was caused by. Then it takes me a bit more to process the possibility of what Ethan thinking could be true...

"OK, so OW!" Says the remaining nurse as she hands me a bottle of water and a pill. I take it gratefully and down the water in one go. She hands me a second with a nod to Ethan so I know it's for him.

"Ow is right," Shaun mumbles rubbing his left temple. "As I was saying before you *overreacted* and jumped to the absolute worst possible conclusion..."

"Back in March, both me and Celeste only sensed two babies. Felix could only sense there was more than one. The reason I wanted to do the ultrasound so badly is the fact that although yes, you're almost seven months along, you are WAY bigger than you should be with just twins."

My boy is looking absolutely confused by what Shaun is saying. He's hanging on every word, looking for some sort of clarity. My mind immediately latched what he said... *ONLY sensed two babies...*

Holy. Fucking. Shitballs!

"How many babies are we talking about here, Shaun?" I ask and watch my boy's eyes grow as big as planets when it hits him.

"Just three, but it means I'm basically moving in with you guys until they come out," he says with a grin. "You wanna know what you're having?"

I'm just happy the babies are healthy, but I am curious. I will leave it up to Ethan to decide if he wants a surprise, but I hope he doesn't. I raise my eyebrows in question when he looks up at me. He just smiles and nods his head like a bobblehead that someone just tapped.

"Two boys and a girl," says the nurse as she tucks a blanket around the other one who passed out. "The boys are likely identical if you had two turn into three."

Shaun inclines his head toward the nurse in agreement and I'm thrown. Two boys, I'm sure I can handle... But how the hell am I supposed to be a father to a little girl and NOT spoil the hell out of her???

I feel a tension run through my boy as he whispers, "I think I'm ready for home now, Daddy."

The smile is gone from his face. He was so excited mere seconds ago. What in the actual fuck happened? I look around the room to see that I was lost in my head for a bit there because Shaun and the nurse have both left us alone in the room and there's shouting coming from the direction of the elevators.

"You're nothing but a damn nurse, Savannah! You're lucky I didn't take your job back in December for that stunt you pulled!"

Ethan is shrinking in on himself more the longer that asshole keeps rambling. I want to go give whoever it is a piece of my mind for upsetting my mate, but my boy has a death grip on my hand. I can actually feel the bones grinding against each other when he pulls me closer.

"Doctor Delphi! You have no business on this floor and you sure as hell have no authority to talk to MY nurse in that way! Get the FUCK out before I tell Edward that you keep ignoring the rules of this hospital that he himself set forth," Shaun yells back at the asswipe before growling barely audibly, "Or would you rather me tell him that you're the one who is upsetting his grandson?"

There are sounds of a scuffle but eventually the sound of the elevator doors closing allow me to finally release the breath I had been holding. Shaun and Nurse Savannah come back into the room looking annoyed but not really upset, so Ethan manages to relax a little bit. I'm going to have to drive home single handed, but at least he didn't go into a full on panic attack this time...

"Is the voice gone?" Ethan whispers, hugging himself as tight as possible now that he's released my hand. "He can't know I'm pregnant. He'll want me back. He can't know. I can't go back. I won't go back! He can't have me! He can't have them!"

Ethan is getting hysterical and I can see from Shaun's expression that he isn't going to be able to hold back the next psychic blast with this panic...

I pull all the command and authority I can from my wolf being Alpha and push it toward my mate.

Sleep, baby. It's just a bad dream.

I push the command to sleep and it takes affect almost immediately... thankfully in enough time to prevent another meltdown.

I hate using my authority. Used incorrectly, it can take away free will and that is the very last thing I ever want to do to anyone, especially my mate. Misuse of Authority by an Alpha is a punishable offense that has eliminated many Alpha lines over the years.

The three of us still awake in the room stare at each other in confusion. I know Nurse Savannah doesn't have his full history, but I don't know how much Shaun has been privy too just yet.

Between the panic and the words, the only thing I can surmise is that that asshole doctor is somehow connected to the lab where Ethan was for eight years... The question is who is he and how in the fuck is he this close to all of us without our knowledge?

NINE

I can smell the antiseptic and the blood and the shit... For some reason the cleaning stuff they use takes care of the smell of the urine, but not the blood or shit. Maybe they should invest in those enzyme cleaners that are always advertised to cat owners... Petey and Needle Dick aren't the biggest fans of the cleanup after a session on the table, so I'm sure they want to make it easier on themselves, right?

Weasel comes in after I'm strapped in already, but he's not alone today. Before I can get a good look at the man, a blindfold is tied around my head and a gag is forced in my mouth. One of the guys fully restrains my head, so I know it's back to a not so fun day. For some reason, even though I've been watching and learning for a while, today I'm back to being just another animal. It must have something to do with

the visitor. Me and weasel, we were becoming besties...
NOT!

My wolf lets me know that something smells funny while I just lay there waiting for whatever is going to happen. Yeah, the shitty cleaning stuff they use...

"I want to see how it is set up inside the body, first," the visitor says. It's the voice from the phone. The man in charge actually showed up in person, but why bother hiding from me? Is he afraid I'll get out and recognize him for human experimentation and turn him in? That is laughable.

Fuck that! If I get out and come across him, I'll just disembowel him. I'll put all of my newfound knowledge to use and bring him to the edge of death over and over and over until I can be certain he will do the deed himself. The G-Lady can't fault me for that one.

"Interesting," the voice mumbles after about an hour of poking around in my open abdomen. "Close him back up. Continue the impregnation practice. No need to wait for results in between sessions. Just test weekly. It doesn't matter who the sire is as long as we can observe the birth and study the offspring."

Like FUCK is this guy getting his hands on any kid of mine! I feel the staples going into my skin while the sounds of footsteps grow fainter.

G-Lady, you better not let one of the douche canoes brought in here by Weasel be my fated mate. I'm not gonna be a papa in captivity. I'll find a way to off myself if you allow it to happen!

I jolt awake with a scream. It's been two weeks since the ultrasound and every time I close my eyes it's another memory of the lab, another memory with "the voice." The first natural sleep after getting home from the appointment, my dreams leaked to Ric again. That hadn't happened since before Halloween, but it's becoming more and more frequent. It's almost like the fates are gearing us up for something... like they know I can't just say it, so they show it to Daddy so he can figure it out.

This is the first time I remember Doctor Douche actually *being* at the lab. It was only the one time, but I totally forgot about it. This whole waking up suddenly thing is not fun when I'm not allowed to have coffee to be firing on all cylinders. There's something important I'm missing with this memory that I need to know...

But right now, I have three pups, THREE, kicking my bladder like they're in a death match. I'm almost tempted to start using the diapers, but I have my pride. I'd rather piss myself than wear a diaper right now, but I think Daddy's washing machine is wishing I'd change my mind. Sheets are getting cleaned multiple times a day thanks to these future athletes.

A knock at the door has me craning my neck up to see over my belly. I stop my scooching around on the bed trying to get to the edge in order to figure out who is here.

"Need a hand, little dude?" Max chuckles as he comes over and pulls me up by the arms to get me standing. I guess there is one good thing being surrounded by all the strong alpha type guys. I can always get a lift up.

"Ric sent me to find out if you want to come to the kitchen for dinner or if you want to eat in here?"

I give him the look that question deserves. I've spent every single day of the last three weeks in this room with very few trips to the outside world. I haven't been out of the house since the hospital trip. I'm starting to feel like a prisoner. I need these pups out of me sooner rather than later. or else I am going to go completely insane.

But first... bathroom...

I barely make it to the door when it becomes a moot point.

"At least you made it to the tile this time," Max whispers pulling me into a hug while I start crying. Hormones suck...

Ric

The memories are killing me. It's getting harder and harder to not go hunting that asswipe down every time Ethan wakes up from a nightmare. As soon as we got home from the ultrasound, I left Max, Seb, and Bast here with Shaun as guards while Connor and I raced back to the hospital to grab this Doctor Delphi person. By the time we got back there, he was gone.

According to Shaun, Savannah, and the members of my pack that work at the hospital, he disappeared that day and hasn't been seen since. When I questioned Edward about him, he claimed no knowledge of any vampire with the surname of Delphi. After I explained who this Doctor is, the King vowed his own vengeance, but still has no idea where people got the idea that this doctor was part vampire.

Bennet has been coming over regularly to check in on his son, bringing the nurse Savannah with him. Between her and Shaun, Ethan is never without medical assistance just in case. We're not going back to the hospital until we catch this sadistic bastard.

"Uh, Bossman?!" Max's voice has a shrill quality I don't like the sound of and I'm up and running to the hall. I've been working on the nursery since we had to add another crib and dresser for our surprise pup. I don't even bother with the stairs and jump to the floor below. My knees will pay for it, but I am not wasting any seconds.

I hear Shaun's footsteps pounding down the stairs right behind me. Before I can hit the suite that used to be Connor's room, I'm hit with a wave of pain that knocks me to the ground. It feels like someone has just clawed out my intestines. I even look down at myself to see what the damage is, but there's nothing there. Through the pain, I barely register the thudding and cursing behind me.

As the wave of agony subsides, I struggle to regain my feet. Shaun limps past me, growling something about vampires and babies. My brain is still a bit scrambled from that blast. Is that what my boy is feeling? Holy shit, I will never let anyone ever say women or omegas are weak ever again.

Clearing the doorway, I see Max in a similar state to myself, leaning heavily on the furniture. Meanwhile, Ethan is panting and crying, sitting on the edge of the bed. He's arguing something with Shaun, but the doctor isn't having it.

"Enough!" he shouts in my mate's face, hands on hips like a mom scolding a toddler. "Ethan Lewis Sinclair, you WILL go to the hospital so that I can make sure all four of you make it through this labor! I need equipment and assistance and apparently alphas are of zero help based on what I just saw."

My wolf huffs in annoyance as the were-witch's arm sweeps out to indicate both myself and Max, but he has no room to argue. I don't push my luck with it either. I'm guessing that was a contraction, the first of many, and from what I've read they only get worse as labor goes on. It's going to be a very *very* long night...

Shaun does his best to cast a pain relief spell on my boy so that we can get to the hospital without driving off the road, just in case he broadcasts his pain again. My phone is going insane in my pocket and Jackie appears at the top of the steps while we're try to get Ethan to the garage. He insists on walking himself. I just want to carry him, but Shaun even says it's a good thing with the exercise and all. I guess the fact that I might drop him with the next contraction is something to consider as well...

"Is Brother Ethan okay? Are the babies okay?" Jackie asks in a small voice I haven't heard from him in months. My wolf is demanding that I ignore everything but our mate, but the big brother in me refuses to leave Jack alone and scared in the house.

"He's just going to have the babies a bit earlier than we planned," Shaun calls up to him, all the while not taking his attention away from my pregnant mate who is alternating between laughter and growls. "Do me a favor, bud and start the phone calls, yeah? Start with Seb and get him to come over here to stay with you. He can call the rest of the people."

Jack nods excitedly now that he knows no one is really hurt and that the babies are coming. Having a job to do, he runs off to his room to grab his phone. I don't hear him make a call, but the vibrations from my pocket seem to stop. I do hear chimes going off from Max and Shaun's directions though. At my confused glance, Max pulls out his phone and chuckles.

"Kid did a massive group chat titled BABIES ARE COMING and just added the whole family.

"Connor is two minutes away and will sit with Jack until Seb and Zach can get here to stay with him. Zach is watching his nephew for the rest of the summer, so he's hoping Jason will keep Jackie distracted. Lisa and Bennet are leaving for the hospital now. Edward says he's already there and will vamp speed Ethan to the hospital if we need him there quicker...

"Josh is... well he wishes us luck."

I choose to ignore the crestfallen look on my warrior's face as he processes the fact that his mate is avoiding him. It might end up a problem for another day, but for today... not my circus, not my monkeys.

At that moment, another wave of pain rips through Ethan causing him to double over and I almost pass out this time. Shaun's pain relief spell hasn't done shit. This contraction is not as long as the other one, but our resident baby doc looks more worried than relieved at that fact.

"Tell Edward we need the vamp speed," he says to Max while

helping Ethan stand upright again. "I need him to take Ethan and Josh to get me. There's no time. These kids are coming now whether we want them to or not."

TEN

Ethan

MOTHER-FUCKING-SHIT-FUCK-DAMN-FUCKING-SHIT-BALLS-DONKEY-TITS!

Contractions fucking hurt!

I'm not happy about the fact that we had to leave Daddy behind, but I'm hooked up to an IV and whatever drugs they're giving me are doing their job a hell of a lot better than my bestie's spellwork. Apparently, my labor stalled out shortly after I got here, which is nice because I at least know Ric won't miss his kids coming into the world. But it also means I'm stuck here at the hospital where my biggest nightmare was last seen...

Shaun and Savannah keep going in and out of the room with other nurses and orderlies. There are orders that no other doctor is allowed in the room, and I'm super grateful. The contractions are bad enough. I don't need a panic attack on top of them.

Grandpa Eddie got me here in under a couple seconds, but the coward ran out of the room during the next contraction. Apparently, the almighty vampire king is just as squeamish as the alpha wolves. The thought makes me giggle... or maybe it's the drugs... or the adrenaline... or endorphins...

Eh, it's something. But at least Sully stuck it out with me. He's staying here with me while Shaun gets everything ready, and we wait for Daddy to catch up to us. All the plans are just blown out the window. They had to turn back halfway here because they all forgot the go bag that I put in the back of the SUV specifically for this reason. They all jumped into Connor's truck instead. Alpha idiots...

The lights in the room start flickering for some reason, and I don't have the benefit of my wolf to fall back on to ask if he knows what's up. He pulled back as soon as my water broke. He's all instinct on pushing out the pups and making sure they're fine. He doesn't care about electrical issues.

"You seeing this too, E?" Sully asks me, grabbing my hand.

I nod and look to the door with him as the knob starts to turn. Every single person coming in has been knocking every single time. Why is the door opening?

Suddenly, the room is shrouded in darkness and I hear Sully fighting someone across the room. When did he let go of my hand? Who came in the room? What the fuck is going...

FFFFFUUUUUUCK!

Not the time I want another contraction. By the time I've breathed through it and opened my eyes, there is light in the room, but it's from a candle... I didn't think you were allowed open flames in hospital rooms anymore...

"Hello, Omega."

My wolf growls but otherwise, I'm stuck on my own. His job is the pups. I'm going to fuck this guy's day up royally if he doesn't get the fuck away from me and my babies right the fuck now!

"Fuck you, Dick Nozzle!" I shout at him, hoping that someone outside will hear it. There's nothing outside the door. In fact, I can't even hear Sully breathing. I mean he's a vampire so he doesn't have to, but if he's not breathing it means he's out cold.

Shit... I'm alone with him...

Well, I guess it's time to call in the big guns and take care of everything once and for all...

"G-Lady! Time to close out this deal, but this asswipe is trying to keep us bound together!"

I have no clue if she will even care, but it's my only shot. Apparently, she's feeling benevolent today because the douche freezes and she appears... Benevolence or exasperation. I never know after the way I left her last time. We're about to be free of each other and if this dick kills me before I can give birth, there's no escape. I can't kill him yet because then we end up in the eternal loop I tricked her with before.

Hello, Child. Why am I here when we are so close to being free of each other?

I point behind her to the man who caused all of this shit. I fully expect her to go all spite and fury on him like she did with the faery prince, but instead she laughs and waves her hand to unfreeze him. What the fuck? Whose side is she on here?

Nephew dear, why are you still going after my things? You were told about this. I need the children first.

NEPHEW?!?!?

I knew the G-Lady screwed me over when she made the deal horribly in her favor by taking advantage of my ignorance. I never in a million years thought she would double cross me like this. Where is her honor that she put so much weight on that kept me from killing all the assholes that deserved it???

Oh, my sweet Ethan, my honor is intact as long as none know what happens in this room. Do you honestly believe that you ended up in my nephew's care by accident?

I guess she can tell that I'm going into a bit of shock because she fucking laughs at me. I somehow manage to keep the blank face, but the rage inside of me is just below apocalyptic levels...

Allow me to show you, small one, how you've always belonged to me. Your daughter belongs to me, as well.

THE FUCK?

I'm thrown into her memories. The images flashing past are people and things I know at first. Then some people I don't recognize are showing up. The lady looks a little familiar, and the guy has the same build as Connie...

"Olivia, we need to go to the Goddess for this! The Welling blood must recover its place in the Alpha bloodline. It's our destiny. The fates have spoken," the man says to the woman, Olivia. She's holding a tiny pink bundle in her arms.

"The Goddess blesses as she wills it, Russel. If the fates have decreed it, it will happen," Olivia replies, gently rocking the baby. "Esther will be with whomever fate chooses for her..."

Russel turns away and slams the door as he storms out of the house.

I kind of recognize the house. I'm pretty sure this is Uncle Carl's house... so that makes this baby Esther... Fake Mom?!! And if that's Fake Mom, then that's...

My grandma was so beautiful...

As the memory starts to shift, I hear her whisper to the baby, "I *won't allow you to be arranged for mating. You will have your true love. You won't suffer like me."*

If only I could give her a hug. Fake Mom didn't get her fated mate... but then the image reforms and I see Russel out at the old gazebo behind the pack house.

Russel is kneeling, cutting himself to drop blood on the rose-bushes in offering.

"Goddess, please bless my daughter. I offer my flesh and blood to you in exchange. Allow my daughter to be free of fate's chains so that she may mate with the Alpha's son and bring our blood back to our destined glory. I offer you my flesh in my daughter."

The rat bastard didn't even have the decency to keep it to only himself. He offered up a baby without any provocation... As if I needed another reason to hate the fucker...

"My son, I will accept your offering. Your daughter will not know the pull of the fated bond. She will bear you an alpha grandson who will bring honor to your blood."

Russel looks extremely pleased and seals his deal with the Goddess.

"Do you remember the words of the fates, my son?" she asks him before he turns to walk away.

He nods and begins to recite:

The Welling mate will bear the one whose blood will rule beside a Jameson.

The blessed child will hold sons thrice before the daughter heralds the raising of the gods.
The Goddess nods and fades away

I come out of the memory feeling a bit woozy as the pain meds keep me from experiencing the next round of contraction pain. When the contraction subsides, I'm thrown back into memories.

There's a little girl holding a baby. She's wearing black and calls over to a little boy. Russel walks past the doorway and closes the children inside as he says, "Esther, you are their mother now. Remember, no one is allowed to know about the other man. Elizabeth is my daughter until I say otherwise, right?"

"Right, Daddy," she whispers, obviously struggling to hold back tears.

On the other side of the door, people can be heard offering condolences. This is the day of Olivia's funeral...

"My child, why do you cry?" the Goddess appears in front of Esther.

"Mama is gone and now I have to be all growed up. Lizzie isn't to blame though, right? It's the man's fault."

"That's right," the Goddess tells her. "The man is the one who came between your Mommy and Daddy. The man doesn't deserve to have such a pretty baby, right?"

Horror takes root in my mind at the knowledge of exactly what she did in this moment. She singlehandedly set my whole life in motion right here... almost completely derailing my conception...

The little girl mumbles her promise to the Goddess to never let the man take her baby sister away and the memory fades.

This fucking bitch caused everything all because the power hungry fuckwad that was Russel Welling was too stupid to just let fate take its course...

Another memory flows from the funeral scene...

The adult Esther I remember is doing the same ritual with the flowers that her father did.

"Hello, my child," she says as she appears with a smile. "What bargain do you wish to strike today?"

Esther looks furious as she asks, "Can you kill the mongrel for me? He won't die no matter what I do!"

Hold up... WHAT? I really don't know if the G-Lady intends for me to see this memory. If she does, she ain't helping her case with me. The little bit of sympathy I felt for Fake Mom just fucking got obliterated.

The Goddess looks like she's considering it and Esther is pacing angrily, muttering about all of the different ways she's tried to kill me...

"I will not kill for you, my child," she chides Esther, but before the woman can explode in anger, the Goddess continues. "I can however arrange to have the boy removed from your care and the world will believe he is dead."

Esther looks conflicted before eventually squaring her shoulders and nodding. "Yes, I accept."

"Then you owe me a child of your blood, for service or sacrifice. If you do not provide, your life shall be forfeit," the Goddess warns.

"My son will be your servant and shall provide you with all of the access you need. I swear it on my life. I Esther Regina Welling Sinclair do swear that my son will pledge himself to you before that thing comes of age or my life is forfeit."

The sound of the Goddess laughing accompanies the fading of the memory.

At this point, I'm truly not sure if the G-Lady is still showing me this because she wants to or if my ability to pull memories has latched on like it did with Max earlier this year, but another one comes to me that I'm almost positive she doesn't want me to see. It's also the first one not involving someone related to me.

"What makes you guys so special?" the man screams at the Goddess and others like her gathered around the stone table. "I have the same blood in my veins, but I get none of the benefits!"

"Darling nephew, you are half mortal. Of course you are inferior," says one of the men at the table. Based on his wardrobe I'd have to hazard a guess that he's an agricultural god of some sort. "Your father, our brother, made his choice to stay with your mortal mother as a mortal man. Take it up with him as to why you are powerless."

I can see now that the halfling man is none other than

the doctor who has haunted me for almost the last decade of my life... But as the others get up and leave the table, the Goddess stays behind.

"Ianto, darling, do you wish to know how we do what we do?" she asks him, casually picking up some fruit before placing it back on the platter. "You love the human's science, right? Why not use it to break down our creations? That way, you can hold a bit of each of us and preserve our way until the time of the blessed child."

Ianto Delphi... such a pretentious fucking name. And the bitch gave him the idea for the lab. She is the reason it existed. She is the reason we all suffered there...

No, Ethan. YOU are the reason everyone suffered there. Fate gave a prophecy to your grandmother. Her mate tried to take your destiny and give it to his daughter. The fates would not let it go, so everyone suffered so that you could be born. You needed to be born and be mate to Alaric Jameson and conceive three sons and a daughter to satisfy the fates, all because they wrote it down.

And now, your daughter will be my servant and shall raise all of the gods to their former glory according to the prophecy!

Cue megalomaniac over here...

"If you think I'm going to hand over my daughter to you, we're going to find out just what it takes to kill a goddess today," I growl out.

Ianto approaches me while she starts to fade away. I hear her say something along the lines of I'll be dead anyways or something...

That makes me take notice as the jackass manages to wrap his hands around my throat. I can feel my trachea getting crushed and I know there's no healing this in time. My only hope is that Shaun gets back here in time to save the babies. I don't want any of these asshats to touch a single hair on any of their heads...

The blackness has almost completely taken over my vision when I feel his hands fall away from my neck. My body is desperately trying to take in some air, but it isn't working. I hear a thud and Sully saying something over and over, but I can't breathe through a crushed windpipe. I'm dying for real....

The last thing I hear is someone screaming for Shaun...

Ric

Handing my boy off to a vampire, even his grandfather, is one of the most difficult things I've ever done. Doc Rawlings has worked with me a lot on my prejudices but in high stress situations like this, it is tough not to fall back into old habits. Luckily, Max was there to hold me back as my wolf tried to come forward in his misguided attempt to protect our mate. It would make for some awkward holidays in the future if I attacked Edward for getting Ethan to the hospital faster.

We finally make it to the hospital about an hour after Shaun and Ethan were whisked away. It would have been sooner, but we had to turn back because I forgot the bag. Everyone told me to keep a go bag in every car just in case... and I did put one in every single car in my garage. Only problem is, we just hopped into Connor's truck when he pulled up.

After getting the bag from a smirking Mr. Morrison, we made it to the parking lot of the hospital in a definitively lawbreaking record time. I'm still trying to convince my stomach that it needs to remain inside of my body as I tumble out of the passenger side of the truck and stagger toward the emergency entrance.

Once inside, Celeste is there to greet us wearing scrubs. Huh... I didn't realize she was a nurse.

"Ric, Con, Max... I'll take you to where they are," she says as she heads straight for the elevators on the other side of the security desk. "We got him into a private room on the delivery floor and between the drugs, Shaun, and Joshua we seem to have gotten the psychic blasts under control."

She hits the button for the tenth floor and I can't seem to settle myself down. My wolf is itching to get out. The need to protect my mate is more heightened than I've ever felt before, even when watching his life directly threatened...

"That would be the hormones, Alpha," Celeste whispers while keeping her eyes facing forward. "You alpha types all go cavemen when your mate is giving birth because you can't seem to wrap your mind around the fact that this isn't a battle you can fight. You have to trust your mate to be strong enough to do it."

Fae knows nothing about mate. Need to protect! My wolf is still grumbling, but he's settled a bit at being chastised by Celeste.

"Why are you in scrubs?" Max asks as we exit the elevator and head to where we see Bennet and Edward pacing.

"Celeste is one of the best pediatric nurses in this hospital, with the added bonus that she helps us keep the problematic fae away from the children," Shaun huffs as he emerges from a room to our left. "Labor has slowed down now, so we're going to let him get a bit of a break while I finish setting up a psychic net on the floor to catch the overflow that Josh can't stop once the drugs wear off."

First thing I want to do is rush in to see my boy, but Edward and Bennet both grab me and turn me around to talk with them first.

"Number one, you don't want that visual in your head," Edward says with a visual shudder. "I've seen parts of my grandson I never wanted to see at this point, and I don't think you want to have your impression of..."

He struggles to find the right words before setting on "his posterior."

"You don't want to have that sight in your head to affect your intimacy later on," Bennet adds on from my other side considering Edward has seemed to stall out.

"For fuck's sake, Bennet!" Lisa smacks her mate upside his head. "If people didn't already know you two didn't play a part in the birth of your children beyond sperm donation, they sure as hell do now!"

The two men both let me go and look rather embarrassed at being called out by this tiny woman. She's about the same height as Ethan, but just as fiery. No wonder my boy calls her his chosen Mama. Her chiding of the two most powerful men on the East Coast manages to break the tension in the room and everyone manages to relax a bit.

While I'm getting some details from Savannah and Shaun is doing his witchy thing, I notice Edward tense out of the corner of my eye. Bennet and Max both see it as well. I put a hand up to the nurse, asking her to wait a moment, and go over to Edward to see what's up.

"The room is silent," he whispers and looks at us all with worry clear on his face. In a flash, he is at the door, but it won't open at all. We all try to break it down and even Shaun tries to use his magic to blast it open, but it just won't budge.

As we watch, the door disappears... What in the actual fuck? *WHERE IS MY MATE?*

My wolf is ready to come out regardless of who is around. We need to find Ethan right away.

"They aren't gone," Edward says next to me, keeping me in place with a hand on my shoulder. "I am hearing some of what Joshua is sending out. They believe him to be unconscious."

I can breathe a bit easier knowing that Josh is there with my boy. I may have a prejudice against their race, but if there is one vampire I trust with Ethan, it's the one who allowed himself to be captured and tortured so that he could try and save a boy he didn't even know. There is no doubt that Joshua Sullivan is a rare form of protector. He will do whatever it takes to save his cousin.

"It's the perpetrator of the lab... and your Goddess who are behind this trickery," Edward sighs as he leans against the wall opposite where the door should be. "The doctor is apparently a demigod. That's all I'm able to get since she's pulled Ethan into her memories. Joshua cannot get through the wall in the boy's mind to see what he's seeing right now."

We do the only thing we can do. We wait while Edward holds his head, hoping to connect more and get more information...

The door reappears after about a minute, but before we can even get it open we hear Josh screaming for Shaun.

When I enter the room, it's like time stops and my eyes have all the time in the world to take in the scene in front of me. The asshole doctor is bleeding and unconscious on the floor by the bed. For a demigod, he must be pretty weak. Josh is leaning over Ethan like he's giving him a kiss. Why is he kissing his cousin?

My eyes focus on my boy, my beautiful mate... His auburn locks are shining under the harsh lights and the shine of his eyes...

There's no life in his eyes. They're blood red and his face is splotchy and purple and blue... His throat is crushed.

"Why won't he heal!?" Josh is screaming. "Ethan, you can't leave me again! I have to keep you safe!"

Shaun pushes past all of us and shoves Josh to the floor. Savannah and Celeste come in and start pushing the rest of us out of the room. Edward and Bennet drag the unconscious demigod from the room on their way out. Lisa tries to pull me out, but I'm rooted to the spot. I can do nothing but watch in horror as Shaun stops trying to save my mate.

"Get the C-Section tray! We're getting these babies out now!"

Josh is still on the ground muttering and crying. Every time someone tries to help him up or get him out of the way of the staff, he starts to go into hysterics. I forget sometimes that Josh suffered in that lab, just like Ethan. This is the first time it's really hit home for me that he's been through it the same way... Even Edward can't seem to subdue him enough to get him up and out of the way...

As Celeste trips over him for the third time, she looks at him and I can see that it's breaking her being in this room, seeing Ethan like this. I watch her force the panic down and refocus, stepping around the sobbing vampire.

"Get him out of here!" Shaun yells out over the sounds of Josh's ramblings and sobs and screams. "If these babies are going to come out safely, I need to be able to move where he is!"

Every person who tries to touch Josh is getting blasted away by an invisible force. Finally, Max rushes forward and manages to scoop him up. The boy clings to his mate for dear life and allows him to take him from the room.

"He has to heal. He can't die. He's not *supposed* to die. It's all my fault. I couldn't save him...."

The sound of Josh's anguish is ringing in my head on repeat as I watch the medical team cut into my boy's corpse to save our babies. Connor tugs my arm until I tear my gaze away from the sight. I see pure anguish in his eyes. None of us know what to say or do right now, so I let him drag me from the room where my mate's blood is now cooling on the floor. Before the door closes behind me, I hear a baby cry.

My knees hit the floor hard enough to cause me to crack some teeth. I'm a father now, but I may have just lost my mate.

ELEVEN

R̲ic̲

For three days, I've been sitting by his bedside in the hospital. The babies are all being released today, so it's our last day together as a family in the same place. Celeste is taking the babies back to the house for me with Bastian. Zach took Jackie over to his place and is keeping him occupied there. Something tells me that my boy isn't coming back the same way he did last year, and I am terrified.

"You sure you don't have names for them, Alpha?" Celeste asks as she carries in my daughter, leaving Bast to carry the two boys.

"My bluebird picked the names but wouldn't tell me," I manage to choke out. "He started baby books for them. The box is on the mantle in the living room. You can pull it down and find out what he chose for them."

I can't even look at my children, let alone name them. I'd give them up in a heartbeat if it means I get my boy back with me. I didn't even get to say goodbye. I don't know these babies. I need my little boy blue... I need my mate. I don't need to be a father...

A growl comes from the door to the room, and I see none other than Joshua standing there. Celeste must have left with the babies already, but this vampire is the last person I want to see. He is the reason my boy is dead. Even with his vamp speed, he wasn't fast enough. His need to funnel information to his king was more important than Ethan's life and he was too late. He was the only one in that room. He was the only one who could have done something, but he didn't...

"If you think I don't fucking blame myself every fucking second, you're more of a fool than I thought!" he snarls at me as he approaches the bed holding Ethan's body. "My cousin should have healed..."

I see the moment his bravado crumbles and he drops to his knees next to the bed opposite me. He clutches Ethan's hand and sobs, burying his face in the sheets... I can't hold onto my anger at him. I can't hold onto any emotions anymore. I'm an empty shell without my boy...

"You need to come back, Cuz. They all need you," the vampire whispers, holding the back of Ethan's hand to his forehead. "You need to be the Papa to those babies. You need to show the world that you fought the gods and won. You need to make sure that bitch doesn't win. Fight for your happiness. Come back to us... Please come back..."

Fighting the gods? Just what happened in that room?

Ethan

I don't know what is more unnatural to me, being in this limbo or looking down and seeing my feet again. I'm not afraid of being dead. I kind of expected it from the moment I had the first contraction. I mean, even though I didn't go out on my birthday, the whole dying in childbirth thing still tracks, right? And I guess this proves it...

I'm not sure how long I've been here, but it's just as boring as ever. Only this time, I don't know how to get back. Usually the G-Lady sends me back, but if the babies are not with me, then were they born? Did they die? I don't know and the not knowing scares me....

"G-Lady? Are you gonna get with it and send me back?" I call out into the nothingness. There's no response. There's no laughter, nothing...

I start singing songs to pass the time. I've gone through all of *Aladdin*, *The Little Mermaid*, *Encanto*, *Frozen*, and *Sweeney Todd* before I feel it's safe to assume that the Goddess has determined our deal is done and she's not going to answer me.

Plus side? If the deal is done, that means the babies lived. I managed to do at least one thing right...

Now, I just have to figure out how in the hell I'm supposed to get back without her help. After the whole family reunion bullshit I witnessed, I don't trust any of the so-called gods. They should all just blink out of existence, or worse become fully human. I wanna see them deal with the Karens at the coffee shop...

"I like the way you think, kid."

Who the fuck is that?

A teenage girl appears in front of me wearing clothing that's a couple decades out of style. I can't put my finger on it, but she looks and feels really familiar...

"Never thought I'd get to see you, Ethan," she exclaims as she comes closer. There's something about her eyes that really hits me. I feel like I should know her... "That bitch that calls herself our Goddess has prevented me from coming through all of the other times you've been here."

"Who are you?" I ask. I'm afraid I know the answer, but I won't say it. It will break me in a way I've never been broken if I'm wrong... I can feel hope in my chest and hold my breath.

"Yes, Ethan. I'm Elizabeth Marie Welling, should have been Sullivan. I'm your mother."

I don't think. I just run to her and throw my arms around her. My mother is here. She's wanted to come to me over and over and over... I can't stop the tears as the sobs violently rip through me. Physically, I'm a few inches taller and over six years older than her, but inside I'm the little boy who only ever wanted to be held...

"Oh, Sweetheart, I'm never letting anything or anyone separate us again," she tells me forcing my face up so that our eyes meet. "I'm going to be a guide for you to help you make sure those babies grow up good and strong and kind."

She pulls us down to sit on the ground... or at least on the surface we're standing on. I just drink in all of her looks. She really does look exactly like her mom, except she has Grandpa Eddie's eyes. They're a gorgeous teal color that honestly looks more magical on her than it ever does with him. He's always too much of a grump...

She giggles and it's an amazing sound echoing through the emptiness of the void. Now, I understand what Daddy means when he says a giggle from someone you love has the power to heal. I don't feel as heavy now...

"As much as I want to spend more time with you, kiddo, we need to get you home to those beautiful babies and your hot as fuck Daddy," she says with a wink and a nudge to my shoulder.

I don't know what makes me smile more, the babies or the fact that my mom thinks my mate is hot as fuck... But she's right either way. I need to find a way to get back home. Unfortunately, I'm clueless as to how to go about it. Resting my head on her shoulder, I tell her about all of the previous times I've been here and how I had to wait for the Goddess to send me back.

"That's not true, though. You came here as a child before ever meeting the Goddess and got back just fine on your own. Remember the safe?"

Oh yeah... How did I go back?

Another voice echoes into the room, but no figure materializes.

"That would have been me."

Both Liz and I look at each other in confusion. I don't know if she recognizes the voice, but I sure as shit do... "Grandma?"

The look on my mother's face at the realization that her mother is here is kinda surreal. I watch as Olivia becomes solid, sitting across from us and we are now three sides of a triangle. As nice as it is to see the women who came before me, I'm really fucking confused as to why they're here...

"So, Ethan, my beautiful grandson, it's time to tell you the story of my side of the family, don't you think?"

Both me and Liz nod vigorously. I thought I got all of the secrets out in the spring, but I guess not...

"Buckle up, my babies. It's a doozy of a tale," she tells us before starting.

"My father was as cruel as the legal mate he sold me to, Russel. He abused us to the point my younger brother actually passed away from his injuries before his wolf could manifest," Olivia says, her fists closed tightly in her lap. "Shortly after that, my mother pulled me aside, on the day before my sixteenth birthday, which is apparently an important day for witches.

"On that day, she told me that our bloodline has the ability to speak and interact with the departed of our family and those who we hold dear, but only after meeting our fated mate. She begged me to hold out for my fated one so that I could find out whether or not my brother was at peace, since she could not reach him. I was devastated that her last thoughts were for my brother and not me. She passed away mere days later from a broken heart."

Olivia takes a minute to compose herself before continuing the explanations.

"As you both are aware, my father arranged the mating with Russel Welling in an attempt to get our family closer to the Alpha's house. The Welling family have always been power hungry and I'm extremely thankful that the whole lot of them are almost gone. Only one remains of that rotten bunch..."

Before I think any better of it, I jump to my feet and yell at my own grandmother.

"Don't you DARE lump Connie in with the rest of those fucking twat waffles! Connor is the best big brother a guy could ever wish for and NOTHING you say will EVER make me think less of him!

"Grandmother or not, I will shank a bitch who talks shit on my big brother," I growl out as Liz pulls me back down to yank me into a hug.

She's laughing as she tells Olivia, "Connor is nothing like his mother. I practically raised the kid from birth until I died. He got the nurturing and caring from you and the strength and loyalty from his father. I did my best to instill the concepts of right and wrong to counter Russel's poison. Took a few beatings to save him as well. He's a good boy, if not a bit blind. But he's been trying to make up for it."

I can't help the pout or the whine in my voice as I add, "He doesn't *need* to make up for anything. He was the only bright spot in that house of horrors and I'm glad he doesn't have the shadows on his soul from childhood like I do."

Looking between the two of us, Olivia seems to be properly confused, but then smiles in the way only a grandma could.

"Fair enough, little bit. For the sake of moving forward, Connor is only a Sinclair... not that John did him any favors by keeping him in the dark..."

I clear my throat to get her back on track. Seriously, does everyone in my family tree have some sort of neurodivergence?

"It's more common with the dual nature of the weres unfortunately, darling," she says.

"Continuing on!" my mother shouts in encouragement and we all giggle for a minute.

"I'm sure you're both aware of the sordid tale of me and Russel and his fucked up deal with that bitch of a Goddess. If he'd only left things alone, our Esther wouldn't have felt the need to have an affair with Dickie boy and she would have been happy with her fated mate."

At my confused look, she nods. "John Sinclair and my Esther were indeed fated, but she couldn't identify him as her mate thanks to Russel's deal. That's why she was never satisfied. She was bitter about the fact that Annabelle got the man she wanted. She never stopped thinking if only her fated mate would show up, she could leave it all behind her."

Liz starts bouncing next to me like a preschooler doing the potty dance. After about ten seconds, she busts in with an, "Oh! Oh! Oh! I know what's next! My big sister got it in her head that Richard was actually supposed to be with her, so Esther did a deal so that Richard would want to forsake his fated mate so they could be together!"

I turn to my mother in shock and horror. My jaw might as well have hit the floor. You're not supposed to be able to forsake a fated mate once bonded! That's the only reason I was able to fully trust Daddy not to hurt me. It's sacred! There are cosmic level consequences for fucking with fate...

"He couldn't hurt Anna other than dismissing her," she assures me. "But the side effect was rather pitiable, but mostly hilarious. In order to get him to want to fuck Esther, the Goddess made him a freaking sex addict to the point he was visiting brothels and every whore in a three state radius."

Liz collapses into giggles, rolling on the ground while Olivia is trying her hardest not to crack a smile. It shouldn't be funny. Really... I shouldn't laugh... It's not right...

The guffaw that breaks through my lips is like the final crack in a dam and the laughter just explodes out. There suddenly seems to be many more voices laughing around us, but the void is still physically empty except for myself, my mother, and my grandmother... the three who died giving birth.

The thought cuts off my laughter abruptly and I struggle not to turn it into a sob.

"So, she *is* the reason for the fae deal as well..." I manage to turn the despair into anger, and it's growing again. "Everything that has happened in my life has all been dictated by that fucking bitch and her selfishness and the so-called goddess pulling all the strings!"

My rage seems to shake the void somehow and my mother wraps me in her arms to calm me. I can't handle it... I just want to let it all go. My life was never my own. My happiness was destroyed before I ever got to have it. I never stood a chance...

"Boy, I *know* you aren't giving up on me, right?" Olivia demands as she pets my head, encouraging me to meet her gaze. "You are a Hurley and a Sullivan and a Heartstone. You have powers that you haven't even discovered yet. No mere goddess can defeat fate and she has decreed the birth of your daughter will bring the razing of the gods..."

She presses her forehead to mine, before leaning in like she's telling a secret.

"Russel never got the written version. It's razing, R-A-Z-E, to destroy. Fate is a funny mistress. She likes her wordplay."

I don't get how that is supposed to make me feel better. I'm glad the gods will get what's coming to them, but my daughter is a baby. What can she do? And how will she be protected until she's old enough to fight gods?

My mind is spinning out, but Liz boops me on the nose and the shock of the action makes my brain stall for a second... just enough to stop the spiral.

"No one said your daughter does the destroying.... Just that her birth kick starts it," she says with glee in her eyes.

"We've got to get going for now, little bit," Olivia says standing up and brushing the imaginary dirt from the seat of her pants. "Call on us when you're ready for the next step."

Both women disappear before I can say anything else.... What I really need to know is how the fuck do I get out of here? I mean ok, I'm apparently supposed to fight a goddess, but how does a dead man accomplish that? Baby steps...

TWELVE

Ric

The babies are two weeks old, and I still can't bring myself to be in the same room as them. When the family brings them into our room to visit with Ethan, I have to leave the room. I can't look at them or think about them. They are the reason I'm empty.

Ethan would never forgive me if I took my pain out on them, so I remove myself. The thought of disappointing him is unbearable.

Staring at the calendar at the bedside, I'm reminded it's just about a year from the day he woke up from being dead last time.

He's going to wake up again. He has to.

I can't live in a world where Ethan Sinclair doesn't exist. The brief morose thought has the little bit I've eaten over the past day trying to make a comeback, so I race into the bathroom to vomit. This time appears to be just the dry heaves thankfully...

Coming out of the bathroom, I notice someone has moved Mr.

Whiskers back to the shelf above the television again. I understand moving him when they do their exams to see if he's healed at all, but they need to learn to put him back. My Blue will throw a fucking fit if Mr. Whiskers isn't in the bed when he wakes up.

I hesitate when I lift the bear from the shelf. I would give anything for a temper tantrum right about now. Grabbing the bear, I sink to the floor next to the bed. The thought of never seeing a tantrum from him or hearing him call me Daddy and stomp his foot before giggling...

I can't help but grip the damn bear with all of my strength.

If there is any power out there that can bring him home to me, please help!

I don't know how long I sit there staring at the ceiling with the tears silently pooling on the bed. I only move when I hear a ripping noise and something thuds onto my stomach. Looking down, I see that somehow Stabby busted through Mr. Whiskers' butt and fell out.

Is this a sign for something? Or do I just need to join my boy so the pain will end?

Squeezing the bear tighter, I can feel something hard inside him. I didn't notice it before because of Stabby, but there's definitely something else hidden in Mr. Whiskers. I hurriedly feel around for the opening at his neck and carefully pull out a small box. It looks like...

NO

It's a ring box.

My hands are shaking as I pry the lid open. There are two rings inside. By the look of the metal, they were made by the same craftsman who made the picture frame Ethan gave me for Christmas. I've never seen such beautiful pieces of jewelry in my life, even if they are forged from scraps.

Lifting out the larger of the two, I see the inscription on the outside reads, "Alpha." The smaller ring says, "Bluebird." Before I place it back in the box, the light glints on an engraving on the inside. It's rougher and looks almost like it's in Ethan's handwriting, just like on the frame. Lifting it so I can angle the light to see, I almost drop it when I can finally make it out...

"I can't do this, Blue!" I whisper on a sob, throwing my head back into the mattress. "I can't live without you. I should have put a ring on your finger last year, but I thought we'd have more time. I'm supposed to be the one to propose, not you. You can't take everything from me..."

Turning to him, I place a kiss on his forehead and whisper, "You can't leave me anymore. Come back and never leave again. I'm begging you. Be my boy forever. Come back to me, Blue..."

"You suck at proposals."

Falling back, I knock over the nightstand and the lamp on it goes crashing to the floor, plunging the room into darkness.

What the fuck? Did I just imagine that?

"Shit! Who turned off the lights again? I thought I made it back this time. Didn't it work?"

Ethan's voice is gravelly and soft from the healing throat wound, but with each sentence, I can hear it getting stronger. I'm frozen to the spot. I don't want to move or make a sound for fear that I'm just imagining this, and it will break the spell.

The door crashes open and light floods the room from the hallway before an excited squeal brings me back to the present. Jack rushes to the bed and grabs Ethan's hand while jumping up and down next to the bed. The pure joy on his face brings a smile to my face.

It feels weird. I just now realize that I haven't smiled in weeks...

The conversation between my boys is rushed and full of giggles and laughing. I'm not really listening. I just focus on the fact that he came back to me.

He's here.

He didn't leave me...

Ethan

Coming back to my body took some trial and error. I would be in the void and then push my way to where I was almost back, only to lose my grip and shoot back to the blackness. The couple times I came through, I managed to catch a glimpse or two of the babies. They're so big now! I kept hoping to see them with their Dada, but he was never in the room when I managed to come through.

I somehow managed the final push when Ric found the rings. They were going to be a surprise on Valentine's Day, but then the whole misunderstanding happened after the warehouse... and then the fae shit... and then the surprise I'm pregnant...

I didn't want to propose and have it be misinterpreted as "Hey you knocked me up now make me an honest man" kinda thing, so I was waiting for the if I survive, then I'll ask him kinda thing.

Ric knocking over the lamp was unexpected to say the least. I can laugh about it now, but when the room went dark, I thought I went back to the void. I was terrified that I would never make it back without a guide, and I refuse to turn to the so-called gods for anything ever again.

With Jackie's arrival, I *know* I am back. Daddy is gripping my hand like he needs to keep me from floating away, but I'm listening to the almost nine year old tell me everything that I missed over the last couple weeks. It's been weeks...

The story about Max's first time changing a poop diaper has us both giggling, but Daddy is still just sitting there. It looks like trying to smile is hurting him, so I tell Jack that I'm hungry to get him out of the room for a bit. He runs off to get me a snack and let everyone know I'm up. I take advantage of the absence and turn to my mate.

"What's wrong with you?" I ask, poking Ric in the middle of

his forehead. "Why aren't you happy to see me back?" I have to admit the thought that he's not happy that I'm back scares the fuck out of me. Two weeks is a long time. What if he got sick of waiting and made a deal and now he'll be a sex addict like his dad...

The chuckle that rumbles from his chest does a lot to calm my thoughts. "We are going to talk about that last part, but to answer your question, I am absolutely ecstatic to have you back. It's just going to take me a little while to transition from where I spent the last two weeks back to showing emotions on the outside."

I can't stop the blush as I realize that I forgot to put up any type of psychic shielding. I got so accustomed to not having a body, that it slipped my mind...

Speaking of bodies, I look down and the aches and pains start filtering in. This isn't as bad as the actual childbirth, but I feel like I was hit by a truck... And I've been there before so I know what it feels like.

"Why do I hurt so much?" I wonder out loud. I don't expect an answer, but I get one from my bestie who is suddenly panting in the doorway. "You've been mostly dead all day," he gasps out between breaths, his grin taking over his whole being.

"Can we watch Princess Bride tonight?" Jackie calls out from somewhere in the house and I hear Max yelling back, "Again?!"

I force myself to sit up and Shaun pulls me in gently for a hug. I know my eyes are leaking, but I don't really care at this point. He's trembling under my hands. I didn't mean to scare everyone. It's not like I want to die when it happens...

"Nothing would heal on your body," he exhales with a shakiness to his voice. "Then, about three days ago, the incision showed progress and then stopped healing. Yesterday, the bruising around your throat started to fade and then stopped... It made no sense. I was afraid you'd heal just to go away again..."

I think I'm beginning to understand what happened with the

healing now. I'll explain it later, but there are some more important matters I need to attend to. Pushing Shaun away, I reach out for Ric to help me up from the bed.

Instead of helping me, he backs away. "You need to rest and restore your strength. Everything else can wait," he tells me.

Fuck.

That.

I turn to Shaun and hold up my arm for him to grab. He looks over at Ric with a bit of fear in his eyes instead of taking my arm. OK fuck this shit!

"What the fuck is going on here?" I snarl at both of them as I push Shaun aside to try and get up on my own. It hurts, a lot, but anger is fueling me. "I come back from the dead and all of a sudden I don't get to make my own choices?" I have to lean heavily on the mattress for the first few steps, but I'm at least moving now.

"If I want to get up from the fucking bed to go take a piss, I can do that, right?!"

I know I'm yelling at this point, but there's a tension in the room that is scaring me and I'm tired of being afraid. I'm fucking fed up with the fear. I'm done with it. FUCK FEAR!

Ric starts to reach for me as I come around the bed but at one glance from me he pulls his hand back. He turns and won't even look at me as he up and leaves the room. I don't want to hurt my Daddy, but it's about damn time he remembers that just because he's Alpha, it doesn't mean he gets to be a dictator. I've NEVER seen his father in him before today, but his treatment of everyone since I woke up is pure Dick.

Emptying my bladder goes a long way to improving my mood. As I finish drying my hands, I hear voices in the bedroom. If Ric is there, he better be ready for some groveling because how he behaved with my bestie was not alright in my book...

It suddenly doesn't even matter when I hear a sound that

erases every negative feeling in my body. Pain? What pain? That sweet gurgle just erased every single ache.

Wrenching the door open, I can only stare at Shaun, Max, and Jack standing at the foot of the bed, each holding an infant.

My babies.

THIRTEEN

Ethan

It took me a minute to get over the shock of seeing the three babies in front of me and not having them jumping on my bladder like a trampoline. How in the hell did these three little creatures fit inside of me? How did I not explode? They're huge now!

Jackie comes toward me first, noticing my indecision on who to go to. "This is your little girl. The baby book didn't have a name stitched in like the boys' ones did, so we've been trying out a few names, but nothing sounds right."

"Tessa is her name," I whisper as Jack lays her in my arms. "Tessa Olivia. The store sent a blank by mistake and was sending out a replacement. I'll have to find out where it is..."

"Oh, it's probably in the pile of stuff Ric let pile up downstairs," Max says while doing a weird bouncy swaying thing with one of the boys. "Neither him nor Connor has done a damn thing these last two weeks and I've been losing my fussing mind over it."

Fussing?

I do a double take at Max's choice of words, and I guess my mouth is hanging open because Shaun reaches over and pushes my jaw up for me before explaining.

"Jack's idea... we started a swear jar to collect for the trips' college funds."

Not a bad idea in this house actually...

"They'll be able to attend fucking Oxford if they want with this house," I mumble before I can catch myself.

"One more dollar to the college fund!" Jackie yells as he runs out of the room. My face is going to split in two if I somehow manage to smile any more.

"We weren't sure which one was which when it came to the boys, so they've become the new Thing One and Thing Two," Max says, holding up one of my boys to show off the Doctor Seuss onesie they put on the boy.

I walk over to Shaun and sniff the baby in his arms. "Thing one is Zander."

Zander is my omega baby. I knew the moment I was told I was having twins that one would be an omega...

"So this little guy is Alec, then?" Max asks, so I hum an affirmative while still watching Zander in Shaun's arms.

My alpha and my omega... Alec and Zander. Little Tessa is also an alpha. But there's something more pressing I need to know... something extremely important. I can't not know...

"Who was out first? Who took their first breath first?" I ask Shaun, my anxiety creeping into my voice as I try to focus on my daughter in my arms.

Max growls as he starts pacing the room with Alec. "What fucking difference does it make? Whoever wants to take over the pack can!"

"You think I give a flying fuck about who the heir is?" I ask incredulously. "In what bizarro fucking universe did I wake up in that you think that who runs this pack matters even a fucking miniscule amount to me?"

Tessa starts fussing in my arms, so I start rocking her to hopefully prevent a meltdown. Keeping her calm is helping to keep me calm right now, so I focus on her.

"We're all going to calm down first," Shaun gently demands. "And to answer your question, Zander was first out, first to breathe. Tessa was last."

Knowing my omega son is protected allows me to relax further. I wish the three of them could split the blessing from my Dad's side of the family, but it's unlikely. Firstborn means there's only one after all. Dad's family thought the line had ended and the blessing or curse had run its course. But then again, they didn't know about me. From what I understand, my three are the first kids of the next generation, so it falls to him.

Or maybe it might actually be all of them... they weren't *born* in the traditional sense. Zander was just the first grabbed out. It doesn't necessarily mean he'd have been first if I was able to actually give birth naturally...

"Have any of them been injured in any way? Blood drawn, small cuts?" I ask out loud.

A confused silence settles over the room. Max knows about my family, but I don't think he's made the connection before now. I see the moment it clicks for him.

"OH!" he says bouncing up and down causing a happy sounding gurgle to come from Alec. "You want to check the blessing, curse, whatever from your Dad, right?"

I sigh and nod. If Zander heals and the other two don't, I'll know for sure he's the only one protected. If they all heal, then the blessing is shared between all three of them. If nothing happens, it may be too early or it may mean the multiples thing broke the chain.

Shaun just shakes his head in exasperation before he turns to walk out the door carrying Zander.

"Let's get these guys downstairs for their next feeding and get you a crash course in infant care," he says over his shoulder. "We can leave the blessing, curse, whatever for later."

As if that was their cue, all three babies start screaming.

Ric

What the fuck happened back there? I have never in my life treated Ethan like that, nor would I ever want to. My reaction scared the shit out of me. He is my mate, my other half. I have no right to tell him what to do.

You are his Alpha. You have every right.

Whose voice *is* that? That is not me. That is *not* my wolf. It sounds familiar, but I can't place it. I think I'm losing it. This voice has been nothing more than a whisper for weeks, so I figured it was a symptom of my grief. This is not grief.

He should not question his Alpha. None of them should. The Alpha's word is the law. The Alpha Mate is nothing more than support for the leader of the pack and the bearer of his pups. They should be seen, not heard...

I grab my phone from my pocket and engage the safe room protocol on my office. Something is very wrong with me and it appears to be psychic in origin. Tapping out a text to Edward, I hope he understands enough to find me help. I cannot be around my mate and children with this voice in my head. My instinct is screaming that it means them harm.

Me:
Psy in head. Blue not safe.

I hope that is enough description for him. I don't want to make things worse or cause this voice to escalate things. Up until today, it was just a voice. It has never influenced my actions until it made me stop Shaun from helping Ethan. That was not my doing. Something else moved my body.

My phone buzzes on the desk and I glance down to see a response from Edward.

Gramps the Vamp:
Get out of the house. I'm coming. Brace
for impact.

What the hell does that mean?

You let a vampire tell you what to do in your own pack? Your own house? No wonder everyone leaves you. You are weak! They question you at every turn. Even your own Beta disrespects you to your face and yet you do nothing!

WEAK! USELESS!

Someone is knocking on the office door, but I can barely hear it over the voice screaming in my head. I need to get out of the house. I need to get it locked down, keep them all safe. I flip the controls in the desk drawer and type out a quick text to Max. I'm almost out of time... I manage to pry open the window enough to squeeze my body out before the shutters can close.

Dropping my phone to the floor, I throw myself out the window to land in the backyard below. I hope the message reaches him...

FOURTEEN

<u>Ethan</u>

Feeding three babies is chaotic to start, but it turns relaxing once everyone is finally sucking on their bottles. Max even grabs me one of my sippy cups and gives me some chocolate milk while the triplets suck down their formula. It's all a nice peaceful time until the slam of the shutters locking down the house causes us to jump, and all three babies start screaming again.

Clutching Tessa to my chest, I run to the patio doors only to find the way blocked by the industrial steel shutters. The only other time I know of that the house was sealed up was my first heat here... That day does not trigger good memories thanks to our epic earlier miscommunication issues.

My panic is triggering my daughter, so I hurry to hand her off to anyone else before I completely lose it. Someone taps my elbow and it's Jack. He just came from the kitchen with Mr. Morrison and his nephew. Jackie gently takes his niece from my arms to allow me to step back a bit.

"What's going on?" Zach raises his voice above the screeching babies. "What's with the lockdown?"

Max hands Alec over to the teacher and pulls out his phone. His frown says we are not going to like whatever is on there. I make the grabby hands gesture for his phone, and he reluctantly hands it over.

"No service with the shutters down, but a message came through right before we got sealed in," he tells everyone. "We're stuck here for the time being. Just waiting on our Alpha to take care of something."

I don't hear anymore of what he's saying. I can only see what is on the screen. It's a message from Ric that makes my blood freeze in my veins.

> **Alpha Ric:**
> Keep them safe. Voice in head. Not me.
> Don't trust me. Love him. Love them.
> Don't trust me.

The phone drops from my hands, but I don't care. Something is wrong with Daddy. Daddy needs me...

I don't even know how, but Sully is holding me around the waist, lifting me off the ground so I can't go anywhere. I'm not in the back hallway anymore. I'm in the downstairs suite where I was while pregnant. I have apparently ripped the bathroom cabinet open...

I need to open the office and the house and get to Daddy. I need to get to Daddy and save him!

"You can't go after him!" Sully is yelling at me. "If you open this house, they will kill everyone! Is that what you want?"

The words finally register after a delay. My body sags in my cousin's arms and he has to gently lower me to the floor. My legs refuse to hold me up. It's all because of me. It's all my fault, always my fault...

Max rushes into the room and kneels down next to me to brush the hair away from my face. Sully looks like he bit into a lemon but doesn't say anything. This right here is another thing that's all my fault. Why did I have to meet Max? Why did he have to save me so many times? If he hadn't saved me, my cousin would be happy with his mate...

Why did fate even bother with me at all? So many people keep getting hurt just because I exist...

"It is *not* your fault, little dude," Max whispers. "Bossman hasn't been himself since the hospital. He never even seen the babies... wouldn't go near them. Left the room if we came near him with them."

The shock of that news seems to snap me back into focus a bit. Ric was so excited to be Dada to the babies. He picked out almost every stuffie and blankie. He chose the forest motif for the nursery. He picked out a different mobile for each crib, saying they may be coming into the world as one unit but they are individuals first and foremost...

Ric would never refuse to see them unless...

Somehow not seeing them was protecting them.

"Has his wolf come out at all?" I ask Max while Sully closes up the cabinets I threw open in my search for the office controls.

The warrior shakes his head after thinking about it. "Not even a growl or a snarl that could be attributed to it."

Jumping to my feet, I brush the invisible dirt from my butt and square my shoulders. To hell with this shit. I'm tired of them fucking with my family. It is time to go to war with the gods.

They could have just left us alone. They could have called it a done deal and gone about their merry way... bygones and all that. I really didn't want to have to go nuclear on them, but this is too much.

My wolf's growl is echoing through the house, and I can hear the response from every wolf inside with me... even my babies. *That* is a bit disturbing, but something to think about another day. As my wolf increases the volume, I can feel the response from outside the house. Every wolf in the pack is responding to my call.

This is what Alpha Mate means, my wolf tells me. *We are one with pack. Pack answers your call.*

Without the use of cell phones, I'm not sure what more I can do to help until I feel a knocking in my mind.

Little brother? What's going on? Connor asks. I can feel the smile break across my face. Who needs cell phones anyways...

Gear up, big brother. We're going to war.

With who?! He sends back to me. I can already feel his reluctance to take part, but I'm not giving him an option. This is a fight for all of us, for all of the supernaturals that these so-called gods look down on.

The ones who made the mistake of fucking with me, I growl back to him and it echoes through the pack.

No one, not even the deities, get to fuck with my family and get away with it. Ethan Lewis Sinclair Sullivan, soon to be Jameson, is done being afraid. This bitch just took me to DEFCON 1 and the world will know what it means to fuck around and find out when you cross the fated descendant of the Hurley, Sullivan, and Heartstone bloodlines...

"Wait a second... HURLEY?" Josh squeaks out. "Who's a Hurley?!"

My vampire cousin looks like he's going to throw up...

FIFTEEN

Ric

I run away to the only place I can think of that could be remote enough and also likely to be warded. I just hope Shaun didn't rent the place out while he's been staying at the house. I almost miss the turnoff but manage to get my SUV to make the turn without rolling over or me slowing down. Skidding to a stop on the gravel next to the shack, I race inside.

As soon as I'm across the threshold, I can feel the invader in my mind being pushed back. It is not gone, but something about Shaun's warding here has weakened it. Pacing the length of the living room, I wait for Edward to show up.

I didn't bother to tell him where I was heading because I didn't decide until I was on the road and about to pass the turnoff.

I can't send him a message because I left my phone behind.

I was afraid this thing in my head would make me order someone to open up the house somehow. Right now, since I left from the office window, the only way to open the house is for Connor to reveal where he moved the release for the office and somehow get that message to someone on the inside of the house, where phones won't work.

My legs can't hold me up anymore and I collapse onto the ratty old mismatched couch in relief. My mate and babies are as safe as I can get them for now. I'll see what Edward says, but I'm fully prepared to take care of the problem by any means necessary... even if it means removing myself from the picture permanently.

The knock at the door startles me awake from the half sleep I managed to drift off into. Looking to the door, I am relieved to see the vampire on the porch, but the relief turns to a burning rage in an instant. Before I realize I've even moved, he has me pinned face down on the floor, kicking the door closed behind him. The second the door clicks shut, the rage reduces to a simmer. My whole body shivers and then sags in exhaustion.

"I think perhaps we should keep all the doors and windows closed for the time being," Edward says as he stands up. "Unless you would prefer to be in some form of restraints for the foreseeable future?"

I roll over onto my back and let my forearm flop across my eyes. I don't know what is happening to me or why. I just want to say yes to my boy's proposal and get married and raise my babies with my mate...

"I don't even know their names..." I mutter before the sobs take over. My body curls in on itself as I roll to my side. Edward takes a seat in the recliner and patiently waits while I scream out the pain and frustration and grief.

"They are not dead," the vampire says gently.

Dragging myself into a sitting position, I turn to face him, holding my left knee in front of me. "They are lost to me. I'm enti-tled to grieve the loss," I growl.

It lacks the depth and echo inside of me....

WHERE THE FUCK IS MY WOLF?

Panic rises inside of me as I jump to my feet. This cabin is too small. I need to get to nature. I need to find my wolf.

I can't be Alpha without a wolf.

I can't be Ethan's mate without a wolf.

"Easy, Alaric," Edward croons, holding his hands in front of him like he's talking someone down from a ledge.

I'm not jumping off a building. I'm having an existential crisis because half of me has disappeared and it's taken me WEEKS to notice.

"Your wolf is not gone, just put to sleep by a spell. Now, put the knife down and we will talk."

I look down and see Stabby in my hand.

When did I pick it up?

Did I have it on me since before Ethan woke up?

I don't remember pocketing it...

My hand releases its grip like I've been burned and I back up against the wall of the hallway.

"I think those restraints might not be a bad idea, Gramps."

Edward chuckles and reaches into a bag by the couch. I hadn't even noticed a bag. Out comes some old fashioned iron manacles that look like they belong in a medieval dungeon, not on the same table as a PS-5 controller...

"I'll make it quick," he says without looking at me. "These are warded and spelled against both witches and fae so they should disrupt the influence of whatever is messing with you. Hopefully they also help to wake your wolf."

In the blink of an eye, feel the weight of them closed on my wrists and ankles. The iron chains in between mean my mobility is limited, but I can only feel relief when I start to feel my wolf stirring inside me. Whatever or whoever this voice belongs to, I hope they know what hell they brought down on themselves...

Ethan

Trying to open up a mind link between pack members is hard. Theoretically, I should be able to do it without having to be a conduit, but I haven't quite figured out how. This is why I'm sitting in my playroom with my stuffies trying to imagine them as our pack and the enemy based on the conversation between Max and Connor. I'm hoping the visuals will help figure out our next move without having to open up the house.

Connie has already called my Dad and he's on standby to assist with his warriors for any battles we may face, but mostly I just want for him and Mama Lisa to take in the civilians so that they stay safe. Max made the mistake of saying women and children. Zach asked what about the men who aren't trained to fight? What about the women who would destroy the world to protect their own? The only thing they agree on is the kids...

So my Dad and Mama Lisa are taking in any families or persons not willing to be on the front lines of this battle. A few of the teenagers surprised me though. They chose to stay and fight, despite their parents' pleading and the warriors' pushing. Even now, I feel the pride swelling inside at their remarks that I heard through Connie's mind.

"This is our home, our pack!" one girl's voice rings out over the phone line. She sounds like Sheila, Jack's babysitter and tutor. "These so-called gods have never benefited our pack. They allowed the asswipes and bigots to grind us all into the dirt and make sure no one found happiness outside of their circle of greed. Where was this goddess when we needed her? Not fucking here. And now she wants to take our Alpha away from his mate and newborn kids?

"Do I need to say it louder? Fine.... FUCK THAT BITCH!"

The chanting rises up in the background as Seb tells Connor that there's no chance of getting these teens to move to safety with their parents and stay there, so we might as well accept them and factor them into our plans...

I'm letting the conversations between Max and Connor and Seb and Bastian flow through the back of my mind while I move Bertie and the gang around the floor accordingly. I don't know if they know I'm still listening in, but the babies are sleeping and I'm bored. That whole sleep when the babies sleep thing isn't going to apply to me until I have my Daddy back by my side. I was asleep more or less for over two weeks. I can stay up and take care of this...

A soft knock on the doorframe pulls my gaze away from the stuffie army on the floor to find Sully standing there. At least he no longer looks like he's ready to blow chunks.

"What was with the color change earlier?" I ask him, not knowing if he's listening in or not.

He is looking a bit shaky but manages a smile before planting himself in the rocking chair.

"You know certain witch families have certain abilities, right?" he asks expectantly. I nod because it makes sense if werewolf bloodlines and fae bloodlines have different abilities, then it only makes sense for it to be true for witches as well.

"Well, the Hurley family specializes in the dead," he says with a gulp. "Technically speaking they're necromancers whose abilities can range from your basic medium all the way up to being able to influence vampires."

"But you aren't dead," I blurt out, stating the obvious. I mean vampires are alive just like the rest of us...

Sully shakes his head. Wait a second? Huh?

"Vampires are undead when we get our powers at sixteen. We still can grow and change and choose to have life signs, but technically we're not fully alive in the truest sense of the word. We're..." he struggles to find the right words.

"Outside of life?" I suggest. It makes the most sense to me considering what he's trying to say. It also lines up with my own experiences with the void. It's a place outside of life, but not quite dead...

He sighs in relief. "You get it. Good... Well the Hurley bloodline was supposed to have died out before we were born. My dad told me that my uncle killed the last of them himself over sixty years ago, but if you're a Hurley descendant then they missed one. Do you know if it was through your mom or your dad?"

I ignore his question because to answer puts Connor in danger and I won't do that. "Apparently Gramps missed one... or rather missed killing one... or not because she died after meeting him..."

I need to work on my cryptic skills because Sully jumps up and spins around like he doesn't know where to go.

"HIS MATE WAS A HURLEY?!

"Oh, Dad is never going to let him live this down... But wait, doesn't that mean Connor is..."

He looks down at me with the question in his eyes. I let the coldness seep into my own. "No one fucks with my family, got it?"

Sully's smile grows to the point I can see his fangs. Vamps are usually more careful about that. He nods like a kid being told to be good for Santa. I don't get it, so I go back to focusing on the placement of the stuffy army.

"So anyway, back on track," he says as he plops down next to me on the floor. "If the Hurleys are involved then there is a chance a dead one could be this voice thingy influencing Ric or at least a part of it. Do you know if the lying bitch had anyone in your family swear loyalty to her aside from your deal?"

"None that were blood to me." I say and then immediately sit up straighter. I turn to Sully in horror. Esther wasn't my mother, but she was Olivia's daughter.

FUCK!

"Shit! That's not true!" I tell him jumping up and racing for the stairs. We have to get to Ric or at least find a way to get someone there to help him.

SIXTEEN

<u>Ethan</u>

Max is in the kitchen when I stop cold just in front of him. Sully doesn't notice in time and plows right into him, knocking them both over the island...

Oopsie.

Connie you hearing me? I send to my brother hoping he's not distracted by anything.

What's up, Baby Blue? Where'd Max go? He went silent in the middle of a sentence.

I look at the two bodies splayed out on the kitchen floor. The force of their collision knocked them both out.

He's um... indisposed? Anyways, I need you to get Gramps to find Daddy like asap like fucking yesterday. I tell him in a rush. This really can't wait if it's what I think it is.

Edward is already with Ric. They're trying to figure out who the witch is that's fucking with his head. As soon as they know who it is, they can bring in another to cast them out of him. They just need to make sure it's not a sympathetic or vengeance sworn family to the one fucking with the Alpha.

Okay this is good news — I think. This means Daddy is safe with Gramps. They already know that it's a witchy thing. They haven't brought anyone else in who can be influenced yet. I feel like I can breathe a bit better now.

So, I kinda maybe sorta have a theory on who it is messing with Daddy's head, I send him.

I know he's not going to take it well, so I need to get a direct line to Grandpa Eddie. *Can you get a message to Gramps to jump to my mindlink? I'm not so good with the establishing a connection with the vamps yet unless they're really close by.*

I feel the curiosity through the link with my brother, but there's no way that I can tell him the ghost of his dead mother hates me so much that she's trying to fucking kill us all.

Yeah, I don't see that going over too well, especially with how his mood has been since we came back from Atlanta. I still don't know why he wasn't there.

I'm still feeling kinda hurt about it to be honest...

Little Wolf, my connection with you seems to be upsetting to the one in your mate's head.

Let's file that under seen coming a mile away, Alex.

Do people still use Alex for jeopardy references anymore? I was kinda sad to hear he passed away, but that's the thing with human diseases...

NEED TO FOCUS!

Sorry, squirrel moment... I can hear the chuckle coming through his mind. *I know the witch fucking with Ric. It's Fake Mom!*

There's a weight to the silence to the point I think the connection is severed. If this were a phone call, I'd be pulling the phone away to check the screen... how do I check the connection with my brain? Mentally, I shrug and proceed to tap my finger against my forehead... Can't hurt, right?

Ethan, son, Esther is dead. She can no more invade his mind than breathe the air, Gramps sends back to me.

Ummmm... Could she do it if she happened to be, oh, I don't know... a Hurley?

I feel the rage and fear explode through the connection to the point I almost close it down myself. Is this what Sully felt when he heard the name? Just how bad was this family to the vampires?

Russel Welling was no relation to that family!

Well, that's the truth. If he was, I'm sure he would have found a way to subjugate all of the vampires for profit or power...

No, hc wasn't, but my grandma was, I tell him.

Before he can react fully, I babble on before he goes and jumps to conclusions. *When I was dead this time, she came to me with Mom and they told me all about how being a Hurley allows us to speak with our dead loved ones and eventually with all the dead if we choose, but that we can only access the abilities when we meet our fated mate... something about the wolf needing a tether to life before it allows death in or something. I tuned it out mostly, but she's the one who helped me come back from the void over and over, not the G-Lady... I just didn't know it was her doing it all along...*

I can feel his entire memory rewriting itself while I mentally take a breather. That was a lot all at once. All of the hatred and fear having to be processed and finding out his own mate was almost destroyed by it all before they found each other. It's a sad Romeo and Juliet style kinda feel, but the old man needs to grow a fucking pair and kick Fake Mom to the fucking curb and get me my Daddy back..

I hear the chuckle before I hear the words. *Fake Mom is going to be gone for good this time. I swear it to you, Little Wolf.*

Ric

From the moment Edward puts down his phone, I can feel rage building inside of me. The thing in my head is suppressing my wolf again, but not fully succeeding this time. This time, I remain in control enough that I'm not thrashing against the chains. Then again, I'm doing my best to concentrate on not moving, not reacting to the well of anger pouring over me.

It takes more than a few minutes and I see all kinds of emotions flow over the vampire's face before he ends his connection to Ethan with a diabolical sounding chuckle, looking over at me. I know in the front of my brain that he won't hurt me, but there's a piece of the cave dwelling human in the back of my mind that knows an apex predator is in front of us and if he wanted us dead, we would be dead…

"Accurate, Alaric, but you are not the one who is afraid now," Edward rumbles out as he glides across the floor to stand in front of me. "Isn't that right, Esther?"

I feel the thing in my head shriek and the pain is enough to make my spine bow as my body tenses all over, like thousands of jolts of electricity are flowing through me. But I endure it, knowing that the bitch inside of me has inflicted the last of her vitriolic shit on Ethan and Connor. She should be in oblivion, and I look forward to being the one to send her there myself.

While I am trying to keep my body in one piece through the pain, Edward somehow slips a corded necklace over my head. The second the cord and the charm make contact with my skin, the pain recedes and I collapse back to the couch. This thing is so lumpy, I don't know how anyone can manage to sit on it for longer than a few minutes.

"I have bought us a small reprieve," Edward tells me, pulling me upright. "She will be back soon and likely her hold will be stronger. The only way she could pull this off from beyond the veil of death is if her soul was already bound to one still living. Before I go back to my grandson, can you think of anyone who she was close to that might be bound to her?"

The more I think on it, the only one who could possibly be connected to her would be Connor, but he would never help her to hurt Ethan, not in a million years.

"I have already considered the Sinclair boy, so someone else maybe?" he adds, obviously reading my hesitance. "Joshua is already covering that possibility and blocking what he can on his end. Unfortunately, we vampires are rather useless against this particular clan, so I've summoned backup for us. They should be here shortly... I hope."

We spend the next hour or so in silence watching the shadows move across the floor. Neither of us is willing to talk or turn on the television in case breaking the silence somehow breaks the temporary containment of Esther inside my head.

The only indication that someone is here is when the door flies open and Celeste breezes into the room, literally, with Felix stumbling across the threshold after her. The door slams shut again, seemingly on its own, and I hear a buzzing noise before the energy in the room settles back down.

I feel Esther start to scratch at the bubble holding her in my head at the sight of the new arrivals. It's not Celeste that she doesn't like. It is Felix. There is something about the lad that she wants to eliminate.

"Felix, are you alright?" I ask him, watching the color drain from his face as he sags against the wall.

"Death magic and I have a hate hate relationship, Alpha. It tries to kill me on sight and I generally run away," he chuckles out as his legs give out and he slides to the floor. "But my lovely sister has locked me in the room with a fucking dead Hurley witch that just wants to feed on the destruction of everyone I've come to care about... Just fucking great..."

The energy continues to drain from the fae lad, but Celeste is glowing with power. I'm about to ask her to let her brother out of the house when I hear him take a rattling breath before it just stops... Did she just kill her brother by bringing him here? Did I bring an innocent boy here to die just so I could be selfish and be with my mate?

Something in the pack feels broken and in the distance we all hear a howl of grief echoing through the hills. The realization hits that Felix was fated to someone in my pack, and they had already met. I just killed two innocents...

"Relax, Ric," Celeste says as she grips both sides of my head and stares into my eyes. She's searching for something, and I see the moment she finds it. "Good. She's still contained by the amulet. That makes this easier on all of us..."

Keeping one hand on the top of my head, she doesn't break eye contact while lifting the necklace back off of me. I can feel Esther screaming in my head, but with Celeste here, I don't feel the pain. I hold her stare the entire time until she pushes me away. When I sit back up, I see her rushing to get the necklace around Felix's neck.

She's muttering and chanting, but it looks like things aren't going the way she expects them to. There's a strain to her posture and her grip on her brother's body is tighter than it was initially.

"Fuck! I need a blade and blood of her kin! I didn't think she'd have this strong of a hold..."

I can see her struggle intensifying. As my hand rests on my leg, I feel something in my pocket. My handkerchief that was a present from my grandfather is in there. I wiped the blood from Ethan's mouth at the hospital and never washed it... It's always on me.

I stand in front of Edward, practically shoving my crotch in his face.

At his look of incredulity, I roll my eyes in a way that would make my boy proud. "Front pocket. There's a handkerchief with Ethan's blood on it. Stabby's on the floor over where I dropped it."

The vampire returns my eye roll, but in a flash the items are in Celeste's hand and I'm feeling a bit of a breeze against the front of my legs. Seems that Gramps didn't want to waste time and just tore both pockets away, leaving gaping holes in the front of my pants. His smirk as he sits back in the recliner tells me it was on purpose in retaliation for the eye roll.

The gasp that comes from Felix brings our attention back to the two siblings in the corner, only that's not Felix's eyes looking out at us. Those are the cold dead eyes of Esther Sinclair. I've only seen this look in Ethan's nightmares, but it's enough to where I'll never forget. The woman has no soul.

"Time to talk, bitch," Celeste says as she throws her brother... erm... Esther to the floor in front of the television. "Who brought you back to this plane?"

SEVENTEEN

RIC

It's been hours and Esther still is not talking. It is obviously painful for her to be in Felix's body, especially since the iron manacles were removed from me and put on him. Celeste promises that Felix's body can handle it, but yes, it is as painful as it looks to have the iron on the bare skin like that, even for halflings like them.

Edward has been checking in with Joshua at the house instead of Ethan because Esther seems to grow stronger if he connects with my boy for some reason we can't seem to figure out.

"What is your reason for coming back?" Celeste asks for what seems to be the thousandth time.

I think we are all prepared for her little villain monologue again about how her fate was stolen from her and her mate was given to another and that everything was all done because of the vampires seeking world domination or something or other.

It's all so absurd that I've been playing the new Madden game for the last thirty minutes. Even Edward looks ready to pick up the other controller but the voice that answers isn't the same as before...

"Just fucking answer already and get out of my body, you damned psychotic delusional piece of shit excuse for a breeder!"

Felix's body slams back on the carpet and starts to writhe before suddenly stopping.

"Oh so the little boy wants to come back, does he? Well, what if I refuse to give up this body and stay forever?"

"You want it? Fine. Saves me the trouble of avoiding my life. But you get to deal with the fallout of this body dying. I figure we have about twenty minutes before it becomes *your* problem when an irate werewolf rips you to shreds for killing me."

His body writhes again for about another minute while the rest of us in the room just kind of gawk at each other. What the fuck was Felix talking about there? What wolf in my pack would risk my wrath AND be able to defy me?

"Shit," I mutter as Edward and Celeste turn toward me. "He's out of the house."

<u>Ethan</u>

Playing the go between with Connor and everyone else has gotten old. Sully has assured us that Esther is contained in a way that we don't have to worry about Ric accessing the house anymore, so I convince my big brother to give up the secret of the office lock. Sure enough, it was in his suite... just inside the closet, not in the bathroom.

The plan is that once I get into the office, I open the shutters on the house long enough to swap out the guard and put them back. At least, that is their plan.

I told Connor that I was going to take a nap in the office where no one would bother me. The trips have been surprisingly pretty good sleepers so far, so Connor suggested I bring them into the office with me. Shaun came with us only so he didn't have to deal with being locked in the house with my brother. This will work even better now.

Cracking open the window, I look down. Yeah, I can totally do this, especially with my super speed...

After Shaun finishes settling the babies into their bassinets, I flip the switches to panic lock the office and the outer house shutters. Shaun looks up from across the room with a shocked look on his face. I see the moment he realizes what I've done.

"Sorry, bro!" I call out as I dive out the window. I hit the ground with a roll and hear his responding "Asshole!" before the shutters slam shut and the house is secure again.

With the cell phone blockers and everyone thinking I'm in there with him and the soundproofing, no one will know I'm not inside, at least for a while. I can go find my mate and kick some ghost bitch ass...

"What the fuck do you think you're doing?"

Fuck... "Hey, Max."

"Does anyone know you're outside?" He's looking around as if there's going to be someone jumping up saying Ah ha! Pointing at me in accusation.

"I got out without them knowing and all the guards are in there with the babies, where they belong," I tell him before pouting, "Where *you* would be if you weren't so pigheaded about my cousin..."

The sputtering cough he lets out makes me giggle a little bit before I manage to shake it off. Now, I have to figure out where Gramps is keeping Daddy so that I can go shank an undead bitch... Can one actually kill a ghost?

I mean on Supernatural, they salt and burn the body. But her body was already burnt to a crisp in the fire, so that won't work...

I can do it if she would ever fucking start talking.

That's Felix in my head... why is Felix in my head?

Long story, but short version is I'm dead...ish. Celeste put your bitch of a whore adoptive mother into my body to get her out of Ric but we don't want to destroy her until we know who has her anchored here. Anyone able to deal with death magic at this level needs to be taken care of and we can't destroy Mommy Dearest here without a name.

This is going to be too fun. I just realized I'm not bound by the deal anymore. I can kill, destroy, whatever I want with no repercussions anymore...

I dunno if I like where your thoughts are at man... It's still my body.

"And I'm a wolf in search of my mate. Don't worry, I'll find you soon enough," I growl out loud to Max's surprise. I don't even give him a second glance before I let my wolf come out to run. The transformation is more fluid than it's ever been and I don't see scraps of cloth fluttering around either...

Grandmother taught. No more naked unless want, my wolf

tells me as he lets out a howl and runs for the forest. Time to metaphorically shank a bitch.

She dies if we kill the vessel, my wolf tells me as we speed past the school. At this rate, we'll be outside of the pack territory in about fifteen minutes.

No killing Felix, I remind him and I swear he pouts. I know he's felt limited and constrained being under the deal, but our first kill since Jessica is not going to be our friend's body... even if he *is* possessed by the she-bitch from hell...

Ten minutes to the edge of the pack...

Hey Ethan? Felix breaks in. *Can you try to not mess up my body too much? I warned her that a wolf was coming to rip her to shreds, but I don't know if she's gonna crack under that or not.*

I stagger a bit at his sudden intrusion, but easily resume my run for the border. Five minutes...

Where are they? I won't have to hurt your body. I learned a few tricks from my Grandma the last time I died.

I can feel his surprise, but he tells me that they're holed up in Shaun's cabin. Oh that's even better. I know a shortcut... I'll be there in five minutes, Daddy. Your boy is coming to save the day this time...

EIGHTEEN

Ric

Part of me is excited to see my mate again without being under Esther's influence. A much larger and louder part of me is more concerned about the fact that she seems to grow strength when there's a connection open to him.

The last thing I want to do is have him in danger, but it might take someone of her own bloodline to take her out, according Shaun. My fears that Ethan is on the way were confirmed when he got through on the phone.

I didn't get the full story, but somehow Ethan convinced his brother to give him the location of the office release. And then my boy managed to lock down the house the same way I did, trapping Shaun in the office with the babies until someone outside managed to get Joshua's attention that Ethan was out.

Shaun and Savannah set up in my office for the long haul and engaged the panic room, not the lockdown switch, to keep the babies and Jackie safe, but the rest of the house and the signal blocking are no longer engaged. Until there's a direct threat, we need to keep the lines of communication open now that I'm no longer compromised.

Esther is looking smug, laying on the floor in front of us. She knows now that Ethan is coming here. There's something about putting the two of them in the same room that makes my wolf want to come out and rip Felix's body to shreds.

Keep mate safe, he tells me and for the hundredth time I have to explain to him that if we destroy Felix's body, a member of our pack will likely die from a broken heart like we would if we lost Ethan.

The door slams open ahead of a giant silver wolf. It's Ethan, but this wolf is at least twice the size of the wolf I first saw on New Year's.

The growl coming from his snout causes actual vibrations of the earth and the sounds of the trees creaking outside makes my hair stand on end.

I don't know what happened to my boy, but he is a mother fucking badass!

Esther looks like this is not what she expected. If she was truly here, I'd think she's about to piss herself... oh...

At least Felix and Shaun are about the same size. He'll need a change of pants,

Esther Welling Sinclair, who is your master? Who holds your leash?

The voice echoing in the air around us is Ethan's but there's a command there that speaks of an authority higher than mine as an Alpha.

"No one has ever collared me, you mutt! Now, I shall be reborn and you will finally die!"

The wolf tilts his head as she cackles away in the fae lad's body. Between one breath and the next, the wolf is gone and my boy is standing in its place, fully dressed in his superhero pjs that he woke up in...

Not the most intimidating look, but impressive that he's dressed at all. I don't know of any other wolf that can shift with clothing.

It's a witchy thing, he sends to me with a wink before turning his attention back to the woman possessing his friend.

The contempt on his face crumbles when he sees the burns on Felix's arms and face from where they came in contact with the manacles and chains.

"Release the cuffs. We don't need them," he says with a sigh. "I want Felix to not be in so much pain coming back to his body."

"You think *you* can remove *me*? That's laughable. I will take this body to the grave since you care so much for its owner!"

She seems to reach for something and too late I notice Stabby is within reach now that she's not bound by the chains. She holds the knife to Felix's throat and laughs in triumph at the fear on our faces.

"You are all weak! Fate should have chosen me! It was my fate, not yours!"

Before the knife does more than a slight prick into his neck, the hand holding it suddenly flings the blade across the room. The look of shock on her face is quickly replaced by Felix taking over again.

"Bitch, please. No permanent marks. A man's gotta look good for the one he loves, right buddy?" he says winking at my boy before withdrawing, leaving a very confused looking Esther standing in front of us.

Ethan moves to stand in front of me and gestures for Celeste and Edward to move behind him as well. At this point, we're all of the same mind to let him run this show. I don't know what happened to him over the last few weeks while he was away from us, but it changed him...

And right now is not the time to question those changes.

Ethan

Seeing those dead eyes looking out of my friend's face is jarring to say the least. Part of me is still that little boy staring into that cold abyss of pure malevolence, wishing that she would suddenly remember that she loves me, like a mommy should. Part of me is still the terrified little boy who equates those eyes with death and pain and emptiness and inadequacy...

But right now, the biggest part of me is the fucking Papa bear that wants to rip her soul to shreds for having the mother fucking audacity to try and hurt my babies and my mate. I did NOT suffer through hours of labor, years of physical torture, a lifetime of psychological torment, and a fucked up one sided deal with a woman blessed with an over inflated ego just so that this BITCH could succeed in her evil scheme...

In the words of the teens back at the house: FUCK. THAT. BITCH.

Daddy's hands resting on my shoulders help steady me as I prepare to rip her soul from Felix's body and send her back to hell, like Grandma Olivia showed me. It was a short nap, but productive after Sully let slip just what my family could do once upon a time, before the bloodline mixed with the wolves.

See, the reason Esther is able to pull off all the bullshit she can right now is because she doesn't have a wolf to temper her abilities. The wolf is a thing of life and its power can't be used to control death... or hers couldn't. There's a reason fate brought the Hurleys together with a vampire.

"Wanna know the secret to our family's power?" I ask her once the shock of Felix's little show wears off.

She tries to growl, but Felix ain't the kind of fairy that's very intimidating, so it falls flat. I figure that's enough assent for me to continue. I mean, I'm telling the story no matter what, but I prefer a captive audience.

"See, the Hurley clan was almost totally wiped out by vampires," I begin with a glance at Grandpa Eddie. I know he killed most of them personally. "See and the thing is, they needed killing cuz the greed and lust for power went to their heads. But one daughter ran off before they could corrupt her. She wanted to do good. She wanted to help people say goodbye instead of subjugating the undead.

"She hid her power long enough to convince a lone wolf to mate with her so that she could have a child. She conceived a daughter, but the wolf abandoned her. The woman managed to find a home in a pack thanks to her daughter having a wolf, but being a witch with a halfling, they were horribly mistreated. When the daughter was eighteen, she left that pack to find her mate.

"She found him and they conceived a daughter that very night, but he was killed by a rival shortly thereafter. After their daughter was born, the rival wolf took the woman as his mate and forced her to carry another pup for him. That union bore him a son. However, he was ashamed of his son being only a beta, so he beat him to death before his wolf could fully manifest."

The bitch in Felix's body decides she's going to try and make a run for it while I'm telling the story, but with a flick of my wrist, she's forced to kneel in front of me.

"Don't be rude, Esther. No one likes distractions," I tell her with a smile. That was her favorite line to use with me in front of company to let me know I'd stepped over the line and there would be repercussions. Part of me really enjoys seeing the fear roll through her eyes, but mostly I'm tired and want Mr. Whiskers, a bottle, and a nap...

"Back to the story...

"The girl was distraught at the death of her brother and her mother made her swear she would only ever be with her true mate, that she would trust the fates and only ever love her fated mate. The girl hastily agreed but was eventually bullied into an arranged mating by her father when her mother died suddenly.

"She spent months being brutalized by the man her father gave her to before a teenage girl handed her a note saying it was from the fates. The woman wasn't even pregnant yet, and she hoped that she would never bear a child for the monster she was given to. When she opened the note, it read:

"The Welling mate will bear the one whose blood will rule beside a Jameson. The blessed child will hold sons thrice before the daughter heralds the razing of the gods."

I squat down in front of Esther to really drive the next part home to her...

"You would have lived a happier life with your fated mate had your father not fucked it all up with his deal."

Ric

I'm not sure what all was going on while my boy was telling the story of his bloodline, but you could hear a pin drop a mile away with the silence that fell after he says Russel made a deal. Up until that point, I wasn't sure where he was going with the story. I kept waiting for a name or something I would recognize in it, but until that mention of the note, not a single name was uttered.

Before Esther moves more than an inch, we're all thrown into a vortex of memories. I see a young girl stealing away in the night, the sounds of slaughter ringing out behind her, but her only thought is that they deserved it and the world is a better place for it. Next is a girl being told by her mother that only her true mate will unlock her powers, but that she needs to keep it secret until then.

I see another girl weeping over the body of a boy around Jackie's age. Her mother is begging her to promise to wait for her fated mate, while a man rages in the background, pounding on the door that is seconds away from breaking. The girl is older now, but being pushed into the arms of Russel Welling, who forces her into a bedroom.

Olivia is marked and bruised, walking down the street when a teen in full on punk regalia stops her and presses the note into her hands with a wink. Before she can even react, the punk girl dissipates like smoke in the wind. Reading the note, Olivia quickly rips it up and drops the pieces in separate trash cans before turning toward the path that would lead back to the Welling house.

Russel is kneeling, making a deal with the Goddess for his own selfish gain. She speaks no lie but leaves enough out for him to believe the prophecy of the fates is regarding his newborn daughter, so he makes his deal.

Esther is kneeling, making her own deal for the lover she wants, demanding the Goddess break his bond with his fated mate.

Esther is kneeling again. She promises her son in exchange for getting rid of Ethan...

Esther is tied to the bed burning alive next to her murdered mate, but all she can think about is that it's unfair that Ethan still lives...

Coming back to the present, the only sounds in the room are the soft whimpers coming from Felix's body on the ground. We all saw how the Goddess manipulated the Welling family. We all saw how at every turn, they chose themselves over the innocent, over trusting fate. They brought about their own downfall and until this very moment, Esther had no clue that John was her true mate.

"The hell you unleashed on me in life is nothing compared to what awaits you in death if you don't give up the name of your tether," Ethan growls out with his newfound authority. "I won't be asking again. I already know who it is, but you won't be free until you name them. I cannot guarantee they won't punish you just for existing. At least in hell, you will get another chance at being reborn if you truly repent."

Esther takes a minute to fully compose herself. She opens her mouth, but the look of resignation quickly turns to horror before we watch Felix's head snap to the side and then his body slumps to the ground, dead.

"NOOOOO!" Celeste screams out as she falls to the floor next to her brother's corpse.

Edward rushes forward as well, but there is no sign of life anywhere in the body. With Esther's soul gone, it is truly a dead body. We lost him. We lost Felix, and I just lost a wolf in the worst way possible. The Alpha inside of me howls his grief for the lost mate of one of our own.

I expect my bluebird to turn to me in shock and sadness, but when I look at him all I see is rage. He transforms back to his wolf and races from the cabin. There is no way to catch up to him with his speed... I have to trust that he will come back to us. I have to believe in my mate.

Ethan

She fucking killed him!!!

I can't believe that bitch is so fucking petty and selfish that she killed an innocent just to stop Mommy Dearest from saying she holds the leash. It's not like I didn't already know. I got to see it all in technicolor or whatever the hell the saying is.... It doesn't matter. What matters is, now I have to kill a fucking goddess and there ain't exactly an instruction manual out there.

Actually there is.

HOLY-FUCKING-SHIT-BALL-TWAT-WAFFLE-SUCK-MY-DICK!

Tripping over your own feet? Not fun. Tripping over your own feet running on four legs through the forest at super speed? Fucking ouch!

"I thought you were dead!" I yell into the trees, changing back to my human form. "Why the fuck didn't you say you're still alive?!"

Cuz technically I'm not. My body is most definitely dead and we need to fix that broken neck before the sun comes up so I don't join the undead permanently.

I pull out my phone, kind of amazed it's able to make the transition with my clothes between wolf and human... I wonder if it rings when I'm the wolf if it will be like my fur ringing or vibrating...

Focus, man! I'm literally dying here... or there. You know what I mean!

Scrolling through my contacts, I'm tempted to send a text to Bast, but last thing we need is him being pulled away from the house right now. I settle on sending a single text.

<blockquote>
Me, Myself, and • •
Need super healing ASAP. Cabin in the woods. Sparkle people shit.
</blockquote>

"Happy now?" I ask before pocketing the phone. "He'll fix you up no problem, I'm sure or he'll know how to at least stabilize you so you can go back to your body."

Sparkle people? Oh, you're gonna pay for that one someday when I tell my sister on you.

I hear his chuckle fade and I assume he's gone back to wait by his body. I'm glad he's not DEAD dead, but at the same time, I still want to gank the G-Lady for this bullshit. SHIT! He was gonna tell me how to do it, but then we got all distracted. Damn squirrel brain...

"I can help you."

FUCKING HELL!

"Can I please have ONE godsdamned mother-fucking person NOT try to give me a heart attack today?" I mutter to the sky as I try to get my pulse and breathing back to normal.

Turning in the direction of the voice, I see the punk girl that passed Grandma Olivia the note all those years ago. She looks exactly the same, even down to the nose ring.

"No offense, Chick-a-dee, but you caused enough shit in my life. Maybe it's time for you to butt the fuck out?" I snarl at her. Her little note set all of this in motion forever ago, but now I'm the unlucky dupe that gets the fallout.

"None taken, *hun*," she snarks back. "But that note was my attempt to get her to run while she was away from that piece of shit Russel. If she had gone to the bus station instead of back home, she would have met Edward at the rest stop. She was not supposed to go back to that house!"

How in the hell would this girl know any of that? Unless... no.

She's just another goddess, right? Maybe she's a fairy or something... or a witch. She can't be...

"Yeah. Hiya, Ethan. I'm Fate... or one of them anyways," she tells me as she jumps up on a rock to sit. "I think it's about time for the two of us to clear the air and get you back on track so that those idiots will stop fucking up my plans, yeah?"

I'm having a sit down with Fate... and she's apparently Canadian... Mr. Whiskers is going to be so jealous he missed this...

"So you know the basics, yeah?" She asks me, snapping off a small twig from the branch above her head. "The bitch used *your* fate to trick Russel, who groomed Esther, who wanted to kill you, so the damn interloper could further thwart my plans for you with the lab, yadda, yadda. You get the picture."

Jumping back down to the forest floor, she circles around me, inspecting me...

"Now, we finally have you free of that pesky deal and you've come into your power, so it's your turn to finish what I started," she points to me like she expects me to just perform on command.

My wolf lets out a growl that shakes the earth beneath our feet, but she just laughs.

Instead of giving into my wolf and fully shifting to run away, I put my hands on my hips and let my inner little come out to brat it up a bit. I'm fucking done with the adulting shit today. D-O-N-E. Finished. Finito. Not my circus... Someone else can handle this. I just want a sippy of juice, Mr. Whiskers, and Daddy.

I plant my ass on the moss covered ground criss cross applesauce and pop my thumb in my mouth to wait her out. I'm not doing anything else for anyone else. This is *my* damn life and the only people who can steer me anymore are the three little ones who came out of me. Even Daddy doesn't get to push back anymore if I say I'm done... and I'm so done with this lady and all the fate bullshit.

"Bring me Mr. Whiskers or you get nothing from me. You can find another chosen one to fight your battles," I mumble before scooching around to turn my back to her. "I did my part already. Nothing says I have to be the one to fight. The note only said I had to pop out my baby girl and I did that."

Sulking is my specialty. I can wait all day for her to lose interest and find someone else. I just want to be able to be happy and healthy with my fucking family, not fulfilling some ancient shitstorm of a prophecy because my grandmother got a note.

I don't hear her move, but Mr. Whiskers is dropped in my lap as she leans over to whisper in my ear, "The note was only the highlights, babydoll. Only so much scribbling you can do and not get caught."

TWENTY

Celeste won't stop weeping. Edward is crouched in the corner rubbing at his temples. Ethan ran off into the night, and my babies are screaming in the background of my call with Shaun.

"I'm sorry, Alpha. There's nothing I can do for a broken neck without surgery and there's no way I can clear something like that on such short notice at the hospital. I don't even have surgical privileges unless its obstetrics related."

The babies start to calm in the background, but there's a new level of annoyance to his voice as Shaun continues, "I wish there was something I could do, but even with magic I don't have the materials or ability to do the spells needed to heal a mortal injury like that. A stab wound? Claw gash? Slashed throat? Those things are easy. Broken neck means both bones of the spinal column and brain stem affected. One miniscule mistake could mean paralysis or brain damage. I'm not confident enough to risk it."

"I believe you can do it," Connor's voice comes from the background. Ah, now the annoyance makes sense. "You are an amazing witch."

"Still not talking to you!" Shaun snarls away from the speaker. "Sorry again, Ric. I'll ask around and see if we can find someone with the ability to heal that, but I don't think they'll make it in time."

Before the line disconnects, there's a knock at the door before it opens to reveal Alpha Bennet. He throws his phone at me before he takes in the room and starts stripping off his clothes.

"I've been summoned by my son. After I'm done with the little fae boy, someone had better tell me why my grandchildren are at home with neither of their parents and I'm getting called out to the middle of nowhere to heal a broken neck on a dead body?"

As he shifts, I notice he and Ethan are practically twins in wolf form. There are very slight differences in markings, but the color and size are almost exactly the same. This must be the result of that curse or blessing or whatever... Does this mean one of my kids will be the same?

Before I get a chance to really dwell on it, I hear the gasping breath coming from Felix as Celeste is apparently trying to suffocate the boy who just came back to life.

"Alpha? Hello? What's going on?" Shaun's voice from the phone snaps me back to the moment at hand.

"He's going to be alright," I tell Shaun. "Ethan sent reinforcements with healing abilities apparently."

Disconnecting the call, I give Bennet a questioning look as he pulls up his jeans. He just shrugs as he pulls on his t-shirt and says, "We all get our own quirks with the curse."

"The damn boy is blocking me out!" Edward snarls from the corner. "When did he figure out how to do that? Even full blooded vampires can't do that!"

I don't want to say it, but it's probably the same time he

learned how to control the souls of the dead and pull memories and all the other shit he's able to do now that he's freed from the goddess's deal.

"Forget the damn mind link shit for once, Edward!" Bennet growls then turns to me. "Why are those babies home alone and you are both traipsing around in the woods less than a day after he comes back from the dead?"

"Too much to say," Edward tells him as he grabs Bennet's head in a vice grip from behind. I can only guess that he sent the information straight to the other Alpha's head as I watch the emotions shift across the Alpha's face. They both stagger a bit when the vampire lets go.

"That BITCH!" he roars to the rafters.

"Which one?" mumbles Felix from the floor where he's still got a sobbing Celeste clinging to him.

Ethan

What does she mean, get caught? Who would mess with Fate? I mean we all try to outsmart and outrun her in the best of times, but to fight her? That's just dumb. I know Mr. Whiskers agrees with me. At first, I thought he wasn't real, but I can see the rip in his leg where Stabby slipped out earlier. I left him home so that he wouldn't get hurt more, but if I'm going to battle the source of all my nightmares, it only makes sense that the nightmare hunter is present.

"Not sure how much you know about us, with your education being horribly stunted by, well... everything," she says as she jumps up on the same rock as before. She mirrors my position and sits with her legs crossed and leans down toward me. "There are three of us Fates at any given moment. We are chosen from the various types of beings in this world and do our duty for as long as our bodies hold out. Everyone thinks of the Mother, Maiden, and Crone or the three batty old twats sharing an eye, but we're just three peeps dropped into the sea of all consciousness and time and told to have at it."

Wow. That definitely isn't what is taught in school. I didn't even go to high school where they teach about the Fates, and I still know that we all got it hella wrong. Mr. Whiskers takes his place on my lap and we buckle in for story time with a Fate...

"So, the biggest thing you gotta know about us is that we go a bit insane if someone messes with the timelines we're in charge of personally," she says, leaning back to stare up at the sky. "The so-called goddess kinda threw me in a metaphorical looney bin multiple times over the centuries because I foresaw her doom."

The smirk she is giving me confirms what I don't want to think about.

I don't wanna fight anymore!

"Like it or not, I saw it so you gotta do it," she says in a sing-song voice before getting serious again.

"So, the bitch sidetracked me for a while by corrupting the witches, specifically the Hurley clan. She tricked them into deals for greed and power and showed them foul and despicable ways to use their magics... all by telling them what they should *NEVER* do with their abilities."

I think the sarcasm there was solidly goo. Don't think that drip could have hit harder if it was an anvil on a coyote's head.

"So, I had to find a way to get the line out that you come from," she tells me, jumping up to turn in circles on top of the rock. "I had to delay your grandfather and his brothers long enough for your great great grandmother to escape. Then, I had to have her daughter meet her mate early. Luckily, that guy wasn't vital beyond getting her pregnant, but the damn so-called deities kept jumping in and fucking shit up!"

In her anger, her foot slips and she tumbles down off the rock. When she hurries back to her feet, her face is flushed, but otherwise she is unaffected and the pacing resumes, this time on the ground in front of me.

"Finally, I got a chance with Olivia alone and I had like a two minute window where no one would see. I scribbled as much as I could but had to keep it somewhat vague, just in case someone else got ahold of it. Before I could say anything more after giving her the note, I saw one of *them* come around the corner, so I dipped out as fast as possible. I couldn't risk them harming her to stop the prophecy.

"I lost decades to the insanity from that oversight," she sighs, grinding the heels of her hands to her eyes. "By the time my mind returned to me, you were already locked into that deal. I had to work with my brothers to get you out in a way that wouldn't disrupt anyone else's fate but your own, but I didn't anticipate you being as well connected as you are. My big brother seems to think with his little head too much and he forgot there's more to relationships than sex and more to a person's fate than being born."

It takes me a few moments to realize she's stopped talking. I mean yeah, the crazy punk lady is all powerful and shit, but I slipped into little Ethan and little me gets so freaking bored when it's not a fun story with voices and everything. Daddy tells the best stories. Alec, Zander, and Tessa are gonna love Daddy stories.

"Lost ya, eh?" she chuckles at me. Her soft smile is unexpected after her obvious frustration, but it makes her much prettier, not as angsty. I shake my head at her to let her know I'm following and I shimmy a bit to sit up straighter so she knows I'm paying attention.

"How does me being connected mess things up?" I ask her and then reconsider the question. "How am I *connected?* I was isolated or just not here for most of my life. I've only really talked to anyone in the last year."

"That's not what's important right now," she says glancing at a watch on her wrist. There's no numbers or screen per se, but there's movement on it. "We gotta move. The bitch is trying to fuck me over again, and this time she is going after Connor and your babies..."

THE FUCK SHE IS !!!

TWENTY-ONE

Ric

We spent a total of about fifteen minutes arguing in the cabin about where we all needed to be. Felix insisted we needed to find Ethan in the woods before he makes another deal with a goddess. Edward insisted we split up and keep me and Felix in the warded cabin where we can't be influenced again. Bennet argued that we needed to get back to the house and to his grandchildren who he hasn't properly been introduced to yet.

I am of the mindset that we need to get to the house. I don't know why, but I feel like that is the only option. While the rest of them are still arguing, I start to remove my clothing. It will take longer to get back in my SUV than it will running as a wolf. Driving, I'm limited to roads and speed limits. My wolf will cut through and hit the edge of the pack in about ten minutes, compared to the thirty or more it would take to drive. If I can get someone to meet me at the border, I can be at the house before my car could ever make it across.

Celeste is watching me strip while the others keep fighting. When she notices I caught her staring, she just shrugs and chuckles. Shaking my head, I dig in my jeans pocket and pull out my car keys. I toss them to her and say, "Just get it back to the house in one piece, alright?"

At my words, the other three turn to look, but I'm already shifting. Before I can finish shaking the last tingles of the change from my coal colored fur, Celeste has the door open and is giving me a sweeping bow, complete with a smirk. Running off into the woods for home, I am reminded that I still haven't heard anything from her and Felix about them moving into the pack. After today, I want them there more than ever.

I don't wanna fight anymore!

Ethan's pout comes through loud and clear, and I am torn. My wolf is urging me to turn to our mate. He needs us. We promised we would never abandon him again...

But there is a stronger urge to get my ass back to our house. I suppress my instinct to comfort my mate and kick up the speed to get to the house. I may be Daddy to my little bluebird, but the only thing that could ever trump my boy is being a father to three beautiful babies who I have not even looked at...

The need to see my babies and make sure they are safe is driving me to run faster than I ever have. I am flying through the trees and onto our pack lands, but I do not slow down. A vehicle would take longer at this point. I don't know what has caused the increase of my speed, but I need to get back there...

Reaching the house, I skid to a stop, scenting the air to see what could have driven me back here so hard. I'm not smelling anything off...

Edward slides to a stop next to me a second later, searching for danger as well.

"We will discuss your newfound speed later, Alaric," he says as his gaze focuses on the window to my office. "The others are coming by car. The fae twins are bringing your vehicle back for you."

As nice as it is to not have to worry about getting my car from the remote cabin, my attention is forcefully pulled away from the vampire and back to the house... specifically to the sight of my Beta crashing out of my supposedly unbreakable office window.

Ethan

At the thought of my babies being in danger, I jump to my feet and shift so fast that I fall over. Circulation is important to keep in mind for the future... Sitting with my legs crossed like that made them fall asleep apparently. But that is not what's important. I need to get to my munchkins!

"We're too late to stop it with Connor," she says as she places her tiny hand on my wolfy shoulder. I didn't realize how short she is... or maybe I'm bigger? Our shoulders are at almost the same level...

"You are bigger. Now focus," she tells me, stepping in front of me and grabbing me by the snout.

Bitch wants to die, my wolf rumbles in my head as his growl shakes the trees around us.

"I'll let go when you're not running into a trap," she snarls back at me. "Your mate will protect the babies, so you can relax. You really think after all the trouble we've gone through to get her here, I'd let something happen to Tessa Macrieve?"

The growl cuts abruptly. What the fuck did she just call my daughter?

Tessa Olivia Sullivan Jameson is her FUCKING name! I haven't had her for more than a damn day and you aren't marrying her off to some pencil dick ass nugget until I fucking say so!

The Fate looks shocked and confused. I watch her replay everything back from the last minute. Her eyes do that weird filmy thing that Connie's do... still gives me the icks. When her eyes clear, she shakes herself out like a dog flinging off mud. At least she let go of my snout first.

"She won't meet him until they're both eighteen," she says like it's supposed to reassure me. I don't know that I could think of any man who would want to think about his daughter getting married when she's a newborn... well not any decent man. Russel screwed up everything like that, so I guess it happens...

Doesn't mean the boy is not gonna be greeted with a shotgun. I know I'm pouting, but she's my baby girl and instincts... yeah, let's go with instincts.

"You got eighteen years to NOT worry about Declan," she shouts at me and smacks the back of my hind leg. "Right now, you gotta run in order to keep your family together. If you're too late, you might forever lose someone..."

With that cryptic remark, I watch her fade away like smoke... That is a really cool trick.

WAIT!

FUCK-NOGGINS! I gotta get going!

I shake myself out, like waking from a dream and take off for the house, faster than I've ever gone before.

TWENTY-TWO

Ric

If I didn't already know there was something wrong with Connor before, I sure as shit know now. His fox-colored wolf is trying to attack the smaller dapple gray wolf that I recognize by scent to be Shaun... his mate. No sane wolf would ever attack their mate in wolf form. My Beta is broken somehow, and I need to step in before someone does something they can't take back.

It has already taken me too long to realize that my warriors can't step in on this. Aside from myself and Ethan, no one in the pack is higher than Connor and their wolves won't allow them to go against him. Matters between mates generally don't allow for interference, but fuck that! Those are the old rules that got us all into this shitstorm.

I look around for Max and see him at the doorway in a defensive position. He might be able to handle Connor, but he's taking his duty to defend the babies to heart. If he's the only one who can stop the Beta, then he has put himself in the best position to protect the future of our pack. I can't help but see the longing look he throws up to the window where I see Joshua silhouetted by the light in the office.

If I've learned anything from this last year and the last six months in therapy, it's that keeping quiet helps no one and ultimately makes shit worse. We are talking shit out after today! Communication is the only way forward, but today my fangs and claws will have to do the talking...

I jump in front of Connor's lunge toward the exhausted smaller wolf and feel the same wrongness that was inside of me earlier. I can't hear her in this form, but I can see his mother staring out of the eyes of Connor's wolf. It is all starting to make sense now...

The force of the impact sends the both of us tumbling across the grass, ultimately ending up in the in-ground pool farther away from the house. The cool water seems to do the trick enough to shock us both back to our human forms, and Edward manages to secure the charm necklace on a confused, sputtering and naked Connor. Looking around, his confusion turns to horror at the sight of the small gray wolf still laying under the broken window.

"No. No. No. No..."

His whispers grow harsher and louder until Connor's screams of anguish are echoing through the night. I have to force his arms to his sides to secure his hands when he starts hitting himself and pulling out his own hair in bloody clumps.

The way he is suffering... His mind is shattering... What fucking mother could do something to cause this much pain and anguish to her own flesh and blood? She fucking doted on him! She loved him! How can you hurt someone you love like this?!

Connor's struggles intensify and securing him isn't as easy anymore. I call out to Max for help. I have enough alpha wolves in the pack that we should be able to keep him secured long enough for Celeste and Felix to get here. We need to banish the bitch once and for all, but I sincerely hope Esther didn't break her son irreparably. With Max and Seb helping, we finally get Connor to stop trying to pull himself apart.

"You'll never be rid of me, Alaric Jameson," a whisper comes from his mouth. "My son knows that I am always right. Good riddance to that halfbreed filth. And with me back for good, I'll see he gets a proper mate."

The voice, the posture, the eyes... Connor didn't stop struggling. Esther took over. The body between me and my warriors sags in my arms and I can feel it. My best friend is gone. I don't know what to do. How do I get him back?

The howl of my wolf is trapped within my body. I can't let the others see. They can't know we lost him. I don't do as good of a job as I think, when I hear Max utter a soft curse and look at me with tears in his eyes...He is thinking the same thing I am... How do we tell Ethan his brother is gone?

Ethan

Coming up on the house, I'm not paying attention to my surroundings as much as I'm looking at Daddy and Max looking way too sad. They seem to be holding Connie up, so maybe everything is alright?

The screech of the tires makes me freeze. I flashback to Christmas shopping... waking up in the hospital... Asswipe Ianto leaning over me...

Before the memories can fully drag me under, I hear the very loud rhythmic crunch of metal on asphalt and it pulls me back to the present. Daddy's car is on its side, the underbelly of the beast the only thing I can see now. There's smoke rising in the air, and something is leaking... I've never seen a car crash before. I mean, I've technically been in one and caused a few others, according to Max, but I've never *seen* one.

Another car skids to a stop on the driveway and my father jumps out without even turning off the engine to his beloved Camaro. HOLD UP A FRICKIN SECOND... If Daddy is with Max and Connie, who was in his car?

I quickly shift back to human and run toward the mangled SUV...

Don't be Jackie... Don't be Jackie... Anyone else... PLEASE!

"FUCKING HELL!" Felix groans as he manages to pull himself up and out of the wreckage to sit like a king on his throne on top, or technically the side, of the car. "Airbags fucking *hurt!*"

"COLLEGE FUND!" yells a voice from the office window.

Jackie's in the house. Sweet, blessed relief...

My legs can't hold me upright anymore and I stumble to the ground in thanks to whatever is guiding things these days, fates... universe... purple people eater...

I don't give a flying fuck who or what it is. I'm grateful that they spared Jackie.

Staring at what used to be Ric's favorite vehicle, and what was going to be our official family vehicle, I'm left wondering what the hell else is going to make my heart try to stop today.

Felix topples to the ground in shock, and the reason why is revealed right after. Celeste pulls herself up through the same window her brother had. "You know, I might have an affinity for fire, but it doesn't mean I want to be in a burning car, dumbass!"

Once Dad and I get them both clear, a handful of the teenagers that stayed back to protect the pack set up the hose and sprinkler to keep a continual water spray on the car for now. I kinda really sorta like these kids.

Was this what Daddy, Max, and Connor were like as teenagers? I don't really remember since my trips to the basement became more frequent the older I got. I really only remember the diner and the milkshakes with the guys mostly.

Looking over at them, I realize none of the other adults here, aside from us four, even reacted at all to the car crash. Ric should be going nuts right now seeing that his precious vehicle was damaged, whether in anger or worry doesn't matter... because it's not happening. Why isn't it happening?

The closer I get to them, the more worried I become. Neither Daddy nor Max will look me in the eye and Connie is just staring at the ground. He's not moving, fighting back, nothing. It's like he's an empty shell...

Big brother? I send into his head. There's no reaction... I feel an alarm ringing in my head.

Con? Please answer me... There's zero recognition that anything is getting through. No. No. No. This can't be happening.

"Connor, please answer me," I choke out the whisper. This is my fault for not running here right away. She told me there was time, but then told me to run. I hesitated. I fucking hesitated...

I don't know who stops me from hitting the ground, but I feel arms around me holding me up as the grief tears through me. I'll give it all up. I'll make whatever deal necessary. I cannot lose him - not like this!

The arms grip me tighter as my wolf tries to howl through my human throat. Our grief is all consuming and the world will burn for it.

"Why are his eyes glowing?"

"Who gives a fuck about his eyes! His entire body is glowing!"

I hear them muttering and talking to each other, but my screams combine with my wolf's howls and I can't stop them from coming out. I stop hearing them. I stop hearing everything except the howls. They're all around me.

My beautiful boy, a woman's voice whispers to me. I can feel the slightest touch on my forehead as my hair is pushed back. There is no one in front of me to touch me. Of course, she's not there. The pain of my heart breaking intensifies and the arms around me can no longer support me.

I fall to the ground, nothing will hold me up at this point. As my head hits, I look over toward the house. There, under the window, lies a gray wolf, unmoving... Shaun.

The tears won't stop. I don't think they'll ever stop. The woman's voice is echoing inside my brain, but it's just wishful thinking. My mother is on the other side. She can't be here. If she's here, it means she's not at peace anymore. So she's not here. I'm just finally cracked.

That's all. My brain just finally decided sanity is overrated...

The world fades away until all that exists are the empty, unmoving shells in front of me and my screams resume.

TWENTY-THREE

Ric

The sight of Ethan collapsing to the ground in a heap will haunt me forever. The sounds ripped from his throat froze the very marrow in my bones. It seemed to take hours for him to stop, but in reality it was mere minutes. At the first cry from one of the babies, he stopped screaming, but he was utterly lifeless in his despair. I wanted nothing more than to go to him, but only his Alpha could manage Connor if Esther took him over again.

In the end, Max went over to gather Ethan up from the lawn and carried him into the house. I followed right behind with Connor. Bennet came next, carrying Shaun who was somehow still unconscious in his wolf form. Edward stayed outside with the fae twins to oversee the teenagers as they attempted to put out the fire that was once my car.

When Max passes the stairs, I call out to him. "We're back upstairs."

He turns and looks at me, then down at my mate in his arms. I can tell when he sees it as well. Ethan is catatonic, just as his brother is. The difference is that Ethan is likely to come out of it in a more unpredictable way if he's not in *his* space - especially if the room he's in is one he associates with Connor.

Fuck! How do I do this? How am I supposed to let go of my best friend?

I guide Connor to the suite of rooms that have been his as long as the pack has been here. Whatever is animating his body is apparently compliant enough to follow along. I get him to lay down on the bed, but that is as far as I thought this out. Edward is suddenly there, staying out of sight of the body on the bed.

"Take these and use them to secure him," he says holding out the manacles and chains we used at the cabin. "If we're lucky, they will help him come back..."

Such a bright and happy child. They were kind in trying to keep him happy, but I hope his ignorance isn't what broke him. They'd never forgive themselves...

I'm pretty certain that I wasn't meant to hear that last part. I know for a fact that Ethan hid most of what he suffered at the hands of Esther away from Connor. Based on his reaction the first time our Blue shared with anyone what happened in the basement of the old house in Ohio, I think a lot more was kept hidden as well. My best friend always had a gentle soul and Ethan felt responsible to keep him that way.

I can't say anything. I also hid so much from him in the name of protecting him. In reality, I was protecting my bastard of a father, hiding away my own shame of having come from such a piece of filth. My boy and I are cut from the same cloth. We both want to protect the ones we love, even from things you can't protect someone from. Connor needed the truth to be equipped to fight. We crippled him.

Chaining him to the bed brings me no satisfaction. There's no easy banter between us about how I need to buy him dinner first or that his asshole is exit only. He is empty, like a living doll. There is no resistance, no life despite the rise and fall of his chest.

The sound of a baby's cry breaks me. I know it's not the manliest thing to do, but I can't stay in here a second longer. I flee from the room and race up the stairs to the only place I know I will be alone. I can't face my mate like this. I can't face my babies like this. I can't face anyone like this.

Closing and locking the door to the playroom, I allow my pain to consume me. How did it all go so wrong in just a single day?

Ethan

I should really paint something on this ceiling considering how many times I end up staring at it with no knowledge of how I got here. Maybe a screen that people can send a text to and then I don't have to lay here and wonder.

I don't want to think. I don't want to remember... not sure why just yet, but it's sure to be painful judging by the soreness of my throat.

Brother, my wolf supplies on a mournful howl in my head... And everything crashes back into my consciousness at once.

Torture me. Rape me. Rip me apart... just bring him back! Anybody? I can't live in a world without him, not until he's old and gray and lived the happy life he's supposed to. If he's not here and happy, then why did I have to be treated like that as a kid? What was it all for if it wasn't for him?

There's a heaviness to the house. The babies are downstairs, along with everyone else. I'm alone in my grief, as I should be. It's my fault. I hesitated.

You were in time, my sweet boy.

I've lost it. My mother's voice is echoing in my head again.

You haven't lost your mind, you little shit. I'm still dead, but our family gets to talk to the dead, remember?

I can't help the little giggle that escapes at my mother calling me a "little shit" but it quickly shifts to quiet sobs. I shouldn't be feeling any happiness right now. My big brother is gone and it's all my fault.

Quit saying it's your fucking fault! It's my own damn fault... Connor's voice trails off with a sad sigh. *I don't know why I believed her when she said she wanted to help me be happy.*

Whatever he's saying is just flowing right by me. I'm flitting between excitement and despair. He's not fully gone, but he's still not whole. If he's here and talking to me, then he's actually dead, right?

He is supposed to be falling in love with my best friend and figuring out how to make babies of their own. He is supposed to be making funny faces at the triplets and making them slightly burnt French toast. He is supposed to be *HERE*, not just in spirit, but physically whole and happy with his mate...

Focus, little brother. I'm going to need you to grab the memory from me to show you what happened. I don't think I can say it and still manage to hold our connection. This whole witchblood thing they sprung on us isn't fair at all.

It takes a second for his words to sink in, but yeah. Finding out about the witchy heritage was not fun. But at this point, I'm old hat with it...

"Try being the mutt I am," I mutter softly. "Being a witchborn is probably the least surprising aspect of how the fates fucked me up."

Before I can get any response, I reach out to Connor and pull at his memory. I'm still figuring this out, but I guess it works because the bedroom fades away and I'm suddenly seeing things through my brother's eyes.

TWENTY-FOUR

<u>**CONNOR**</u>

TWO HOURS EARLIER

Grabbing my third cup of coffee for the day I can't help but wonder for the millionth time; how in the fuck am I an uncle to those three adorable babies? They are beautiful just like their papa was. I remember the day Mom and Dad brought him home and I fell in love. It's the same with these three. Instantaneous love.

It is the same with Shaun. I always liked it when he would gatecrash with Ethan at the diner. There was always something about the little shit that made me smile. Right around the time I turned eighteen, I started to feel jealous of my little brother, so I distanced myself.

Then, we lost Ethan and Shaun became a constant reminder of what I lost, not just when I saw him, but every time I got an email, or a letter, or a voicemail... He didn't give up for over eight years. My hope crumbled and disappeared practically immediately, but Shaun wouldn't let me forget.

Had I not ignored him, run from him, I would have known my mate years ago. Shaun has always been the one I love, and I don't deserve him.

You're right, son.

What in the fuck? I know it's been difficult this last year with reconciling who my mother actually was with the woman who raised me, but I didn't think it would make me go insane...

You aren't insane. I came back to you, my little love. The Goddess has given us a chance to make things right.

I know I shouldn't trust the Goddess after everything she put Ethan through, but for the longest time, she was his only solace. She came to his rescue in Atlanta, or so everyone says. Maybe she is trying to make things right, like Mom says.

"What do you want, Mother?" I whisper staring at the floor.

Only to be a part of you again, my sweet boy. Mama knows best what is good for you. You have been miserable for too long now, and I'm going to make it all better now.

The thought of surrendering my pain to this woman, to my Mama, is tempting. In my mind, I know it's absolutely wrong. This woman was a monster to an innocent baby for my entire life, and I never knew. Letting her anywhere near any of us would be disastrous. My mind knows this, but my heart falters for just a second...

That second is all she needs apparently, as suddenly it's like I'm stuck in my ability, only instead of looking and hearing out of someone else's head, it's my own. I am no longer in control of my body, speech, actions...

Walking past Seb and Bastian, I'm screaming in my head that it's not me. They need to stop me! My body is heading for the

186

office where the babies are. I struggle and scream, but it does no good. My hand reaches up to knock on the door.

Please don't answer. Please keep me out. I don't know what she'll do. Please hate me enough to keep me out...

I hear the lock disengage and I try so hard to get my legs to turn away. I try to reach my wolf to shift us so we can run... He's not responding. He can't hear me either. I've never felt fear like this before, but my body is calm.

The door opens to reveal Savannah, the nurse from the Heartstone pack. I forgot she was visiting to help out. This is not good. She doesn't know me enough to know I'm not me...

She's saying something about the babies doing well and she points out who is who, but I don't hear it. I vaguely recollect that we couldn't figure out the names Ethan wanted to use for which babies, but it's irrelevant. I can feel my mother's sinister aura rising inside of my body. She means to harm the babies, and there is nothing I can do to stop her.

The sound of the bathroom door opening pulls our attention away from the babies. Shaun emerges, wiping his hands on his pants and looks at me. I see the disgust on his face morph into pure terror. He sees it.

Someone has seen it... My mate, even through his hatred of me, knows when I am not myself.

The brief flash of joy brings my wolf to the surface. He doesn't understand where the threat is. Somehow my mother has his senses blocked, but he recognizes my fear and shifts us. I try to get through to him, make him understand.

We can't be shifted around the babies! They're too small!

My wolf isn't hearing me. She's blinded him and he's feral. I am not in control. There is only a wild beast on the loose in this locked room with my brother's three beautiful, innocent babies. I scream and scream to whoever might hear me.

Joshua! Edward! Ethan! Someone? Stop me before I kill them all!

Savannah shifts first and although she's strong for a she-wolf, she's no match for the Beta of the pack. As my wolf knocks her out, he loses interest. I heave a sigh of relief that he decided not to kill her.

She would be a fine match for you if she was a higher ranking bloodline. My mother's voice sends a shiver through my spirit. My wolf isn't feral, not truly. My mother is guiding him, influencing him. This is so much worse...

Shaun is suddenly between me and the bassinets.

"Connor, I need you to take back control," he whispers, maintaining eye contact with my wolf. "I can help, but I need you to be in this fight. You can't give up like you gave up on Ethan."

His words strike the final blow. The flash of guilt and pain are enough for my mother to wrest complete control and the last hold I had on my body is gone. I can do nothing but watch from the outside as my wolf rakes his claws down the side of our mate who is shielding our niece with his own body.

I'm trying to grab my wolf, to restrain him, but I have no physical form to get a grip on him. Something I'm doing works, or perhaps he senses I'm not with him, because he backs away shaking his snout as if trying to dislodge something. Or maybe, the scent of our mate's blood is trying to break through my mother's hold on him...

Shaun takes advantage and flings an arm out, sending my wolf through the window to the yard below. I watch my mate shift into a beautiful dapple gray wolf. He's limping and the claw marks have barely stopped bleeding, but he glances my way before leaping through the opening to fight his mate.

If I can't bring you back, don't blame yourself. Maybe in the next life we can get an honest chance.

Did I just get a mind to mind message from Shaun? I thought only the vampires could do it...

Did he say next life?!

No! No! No!

I force my spirit outside and see my wolf being tackled by Alaric. Finally, there is someone here that can subdue me without getting injured. I fly toward my body and manage to make contact just as we hit the water of the pool. The shock of the water is enough to get me back inside.

Now, I just need to regain control.

Feeling a charm lay heavy over my chest, I know I've almost got it. I can't sense my mother at all, but I'm still not fully in the driver's seat. I'm not fully reintegrated with my body just yet. I need something else.

I look for Shaun; he'll know what I need...

"No. No. No. No..."

I leave my body again. I can't handle this. I tried to kill him. He's not moving. I might have killed my mate. I tried to kill babies...

You will do better. No son of mine will be with a half-breed mongrel.

In my despair, I drift farther away. I don't deserve this family. I'm only going to hurt them if I stay. The world fades away to pure blackness, but my grief doesn't dissipate at all. It's only intensified.

"Well *you* aren't supposed to be here," says a somewhat familiar voice behind me.

Turning around, I'm thrown back to being five years old... "Auntie Lizzie?!"

TWENTY-FIVE

<u>*Ethan*</u>

"So what you're saying is Fake Mom pushed you out of your own head and now she's figured out a way to prevent you from getting back to your body?" I ask just to make sure I got the details down. I'm not even approaching the mate and my best friend almost dying thing. That is going to be their thing to work out.

I can feel the affirmation from both Mom and Connor, so I try to think of what can be done at this point. With Shaun out of commission, I don't have any witchy connections to straighten this out.

Maybe Mr. Morrison would know someone? They were room-mates for a while, so he might know...

Grandpa Eddie! *Gramps, do you know a witch who could help put a soul back in a body?*

In a flash, the man in question is at the door to my room.

"Thank the gods you're back!" he breathes out as he rushes to kneel by the bed. "You have been but an empty shell for the last two hours."

"Don't ever thank those bastards again," I growl at him. "They caused all of this and I will destroy each and every one who had a hand in our suffering."

The look of shock and horror on his face would be comical if I wasn't in a hurry to get my brother back in his body. I need my big brother and my werewitch bestie. Hells, I need my whole family for this fight.

A knock at the door pulls my attention away from the unmoving vampire to reveal the fae twins standing there. Celeste pushes Felix into the room. He stumbles over his own feet and faceplants on the foot of the bed.

I'm finally starting to understand what he meant when he said that twins in the fae are always unequal. Celeste is obviously the more powerful of the two, but I find that I'm feeling connected to Felix more and more as time passes.

"Tell him, you dolt!" she hisses out before turning back down the hall. "I'm going back to helping the teens."

At my quizzical look, Felix sighs. The sound brings Gramps out of his frozen funk enough where the fae looks like he's been put under a microscope.

"Tell him what?" Grandpa Eddie snarls.

Felix looks like he's going to be sick, but he manages to mutter, "I might be able to help get Connor back in his body as long as we can gather his soul by sunrise."

That's right! This is Felix's specialty! Or at least he did it himself earlier with his own body.

Jumping out of the bed, I race over to the calendar that Ric put on top of the dresser. It has funny sayings and quotes, but each day also gives the times for sunrise and sunset. I don't even know what day today is, but we got less than an hour either way.

"Connie, you better not drift away again or I'll kill you for real," I growl to the room as I grab Felix by the arm and zoom him down to the suite.

I'm here and ready to try anything, my brother's voice rings in my head while I am looking down at the body on the bed. It's breathing, but it isn't alive.

Felix still looks a bit green, but straightens up and says, "Connor, if you're here I want you to push into your body and not fight me when I come in. I'm gonna pull you out into my body so you can see how I connect and then you should be able to do it yourself, okay?"

There's no warning before Felix's body crumbles to the floor. From the kitchen, I hear a glass shatter, but I ignore it. I'm using all of my energy to wish this wacky plan of ours to be successful.

"This is weird," says the body on the floor. It's not Felix speaking. "I think I got it now, but you're going to have to throw me out. I don't want to know how to astral project on my own, thank you very much."

The body goes back to stillness for a few seconds before Felix sits up, rubbing the newly formed bump on his head. "I always forget to lay down first. Usually, my energy is sapped and I am already at least sitting down first before I jump ship."

A groan from the bed pulls both of our attention. I race to the side of the bed and see Connor at home in his own eyes. My relief is short lived though when he grunts out, "It's not... going to hold. I'm sorry, Blue."

"No. No. No. No," I can't seem to stop the tears. I am not strong enough to say goodbye. I have grieved the loss of my big brother too many times, but never said goodbye. I can't let him go. I won't let him go!

"You can't fight this for me, little brother," Connor whispers as a single tear rolls down to the pillow beneath his head. "Tell Shaun I'm sorry for me? Maybe now he can be happy again."

"Fuck you and your apologies, you self-centered alpha prick!"

I nearly fall off the bed trying to turn to the door and the voice that growled into the room. My best friend is there, barely standing, holding a bloody towel to his side and wearing a pair of sweats that are at least three sizes too big. Letting go of the doorframe, he almost crashes to the floor. Only Felix's quick reflexes manage to keep Shaun upright.

The light in Connor's eyes grows stronger with each step closer Shaun gets to the bed. I try to hold back the hope I'm feeling inside, but could the answer to this problem be the mate bond?

"You have to bite him, Connie!" I blurt out uncontrollably. My damn little side is taking over at the worst possible time, but the excitement and hope brings it out of me. "Bite him and we can all be family forever!"

The horror on my brother's face makes me giggle, but only because Shaun weakly shoves me out of the way with a chuckle of his own. "Keep it down, Brat. We don't need the whole house to know."

Shaun lays down next to Connor on the bed and the two have a whispered and heated conversation. I can't tell if they're getting mad at each other or just turned on, but glancing at the alarm clock on the dresser, I don't give a shit.

"We got less than five minutes until sunrise, so whatever you're doing you gotta do it now," I say, unable to hide my anxiety. I don't know what the issue is, but it can't be big enough to mean losing the most important person in my life, well one of them. I can't lose my big brother, not now...

"I'm not sealing the bond when we don't know if it will even work!" Connor shouts, showing more animation than he has since Christmas, if I'm being honest. His voice is barely a whisper as he mumbles, "I can't be the reason you die as well. Bonded mates never survive the death of the other."

Shaun grips Connor's face and forces their eyes to meet. "We are fated. The bite is just to tie our bodies together." Connor manages to pull his face from his mate's hands and stares at the wall... "I won't kill you..."

Looking at the clock, we're running out of time. I'm bouncing in my anxiety and my thumb is in my mouth. Felix grabs my other hand and we're holding on to each other for dear life. I'm begging Connor to just do it in my head, but he's blocked me out. Why does he want to leave us? Why doesn't he want to be part of my family anymore?

Shaun's growl shakes the room and I hear the babies waking up somewhere in the house as a result.

"IF YOU WON'T DO IT, THEN I WILL!"

I hold my breath until I almost pass out while Shaun wrenches Connor's head to the side and latches onto his neck. It's barbaric and outdated to force a mate mark on another, but it's not unheard of. Ric did it for me. If it saves my brother's life, I don't really give two fucks what anyone says.

I finally exhale when Shaun stands back up, wiping the little trace of blood off of his chin. I expect him to say something or do something to show his love, but he just turns and walks out the door. From the hallway, we hear him mutter, "You'll live, you bastard. At least you'll live."

TWENTY-SIX

Ric

I'm not sure how long I've been crying on the floor of my boy's playroom, but when a growl I don't recognize shakes the entire damn house, I run for the babies. I can already hear them stirring and I've already left Josh alone with them for too long.

When I hit the base of the stairs, I can already hear the argument between Max and his mate spilling into the hallway.

"I don't care what was heard or felt! I finally got them back to sleep and no growl or overbearing oaf is going to interrupt their nap!"

"You don't think you're interrupting with your screeching here?"

I stumble at those words. Max is not going to be able to take that one back.

Turning down the hallway to my office, I hear the slap echo before the slam of a door. Clearing the corner, I see my head warrior on his ass, holding his cheek. I offer a hand up when I reach him, but he doesn't need me to know he fucked up.

Are the babies alright? I send to Josh, knowing he's not likely to open the door to anyone anytime soon.

I can hear the sniffle in his thoughts when he replies.

Tessa is fully awake, but the boys are back to sleep already. I don't know who the growl belonged to, but I do know they're on our side... or specifically on Ethan's. Whoever it was isn't part of any bond outside of their connection to my cousin.

Max still looks dazed, but he heads back to the main part of the house at my indication. We're going to need coffee now that the sun has broken the horizon.

Keep them safe and let me know if you need me or a reprieve, I send to the vampire in my office.

Never thought I would get to the point where I feel safer with a vampire watching my children than I do their own blood uncle...

Speaking of Connor, I should probably check in on him, but the wave of sorrow I feel at the thought of looking into those empty eyes...

Coffee first.

Yes, I'm being a fucking coward. I don't care. Doc Rawlings is going to be getting a huge bonus thanks to the events of the last forty-eight hours. At least this time, I'll have someone to help me through the grieving process the right way...

When Max and I enter the kitchen, Shaun comes in from the other side, from the direction of the suite. He looks absolutely wrecked, and I don't mean just physically. His bare torso shows multiple scars, some quite fresh, but the still bleeding gashes in his side are worrisome to me. I rush forward and support him before he falls over.

He looks longingly at the coffee maker across the room. Max

was already over there, so at my nod, he grabs a third cup for the werewitch.

"What's your poison?" he asks while my cup is pouring out of the machine into my "Not The Mama" mug. My bluebird loves finding things that say I'm a Daddy without fully advertising it. I still have to conduct some business over video and some of the people I deal with would accept the werewolf part, but would run screaming from the idea of anything less than vanilla in the rest of my life.

The witch in my arms takes a long time to respond, but finally mutters, "Make whatever you'd make for Ethan if he was in my shoes. I've made enough decisions for today."

At that, the boy's tears start to fall and the strength in his legs gives out completely. I gently lift him into my arms and carry him to the living room.

This man has sacrificed so much for my boy, my family...

Who am I kidding? This boy IS family. I don't know why he's falling apart. The last time was because of Connor and we needed him to settle Shaun down.

What do I do if he loses it again?

I don't even want to think about it as I lay the gently weeping boy on the sofa, covering him with the blanket. I'm not sure he's even fully awake at this point.

"Thank you for catching him, Daddy," I hear whispered from the doorway. My boy is standing there with a relieved look on his face. "He did something he can't take back, but it's a good thing. I know it is."

At my quizzical look, Ethan walks to me and wraps his arms around my middle. As my arms go back around him, the world feels right for the first time in a very long time.

"He's officially family now, and Connor will just have to live with it," he mutters, burying his face in my chest. "Let's go see our babies and then take a nap, okay Daddy?"

That sounds like a terrific plan to me.

Ethan

Connor is safe. I just have to remember that. My big brother is alive. He might be a sobbing mess that I have no clue how to help, but at least he's here.

Felix squeezes my shoulder as he goes to leave us alone. "I'll go help Josh with the babies. Be patient with him. He has got a lot wrong going on up in there," he says pointing to his own head. I nod as Felix closes the door behind him. It's beyond time to stop keeping things from my big brother.

"Big Brother?" I prod as I climb up onto the bed with him again. "I'm sorry I kept secrets."

I feel his body freeze in place behind me. I can't get through this if I see his disappointment, so I let it all out in a rush while staring at the clock on the dresser. I tell him about my earliest memories of the fear and loneliness, of how him handing me Mr. Whiskers for the first time is my happiest memory. My big brother gave me my protector for when he wasn't around, and it made everything else a bit easier to handle.

I told him about how I was basically a slave to that woman from the time I could walk. I told him how his father tried, but would never go against his mate outright. I told him they were fated mates, but she didn't know it and it distorted their whole bond.

"Can we please save the mate discussions for later?" he interrupts with a whimper. "Please? I want to know more about my father's part in everything eventually but please no more talk of mates..."

The last words are so broken that I just know if I look back, I'll see tears falling. I don't want to see it, so I keep staring at the clock. The words spew out of me for what seems like hours. But it isn't hours. It's barely ten minutes before I hear the mumbled, "Enough."

I turn around to see my big strong alpha big brother curled into a fetal position as much as the chains will allow. I hate to keep him chained up, but it is safer this way at least until I take care of Esther and the goddess for good. I run my hand down his back and lean in to place a kiss on his cheek. I try to ignore the taste of salt on my lips...

"I'll let you get some rest, then" I start walking to the door, praying to whoever or whatever out there that is listening that he will recover from this.

"Ethan?"

"Yeah, Connie?" I turn as I open the door.

"Don't let him blame himself. Don't let him run and hide again... If not for me, then for the babies and you. You need your best friend by your side again. For now and always."

I nod to acknowledge his words, but I don't agree with what he's hinting. Both of them are going to be by my side forever and always. Shaun made his claim. I'll let the dunce recover for a few days before I slap the shit out of him to make him reciprocate. They belong together, just like me and Daddy.

Following the scent of chocolate and ginger, I find Daddy in the living room pulling a blanket over Shaun's sleeping form on the sofa. I go in for a hug and suggest a nap. Thankfully, Daddy agrees. Collapsing into our bed for a couple hours sounds like a really good plan. It's been over twenty four hours since I came back from the dead and I need at least some sleep to function.

Tucking myself into Daddy's arms, I start to doze off staring at the video monitor showing our beautiful babies in the office, watching Jackie and Josh making funny faces at Alec and Tessa while Felix is doing a silly dance with Zander in his arms.

Sleep well, chosen one. The real battle begins when you wake up.

Fuck you, too, Fate. I'm too tired for your shit right now... I finally drift off to dreamland to the sound of her laughter.

TWENTY-SEVEN

Ric

Being awake for so long means that my body succumbs to its exhaustion the second my head hits the pillow. I'm only able to relax enough to get to a deep sleep because I feel my boy in my arms and hear the sounds of our family playing with the babies through the monitor. I almost swear I hear a strange woman's laughter, but I dismiss it. No one is getting to my family.

I become aware of three things almost immediately. Number one, I am not awake. The colors I'm seeing, although natural, are too vibrant to be real. I know this forest like the back of my hand and there is never enough light to get the leaves that green or the brown of the earth that rich. Number two, I don't have my wolf with me. And Number three, I am not alone.

I turn around ready to fight off whoever has dragged me here to see my boy glaring at a young woman dressed in full sixties punk regalia, complete with nose ring and pink Mohawk. Considering they are about the same size, I can understand her lack of worry at his irritation, but something about her causes a shiver to run down my spine. It takes a second for me to hear what Ethan is snarling at her.

"...like I care? You're Fate. You *make* the fucking rules! Why drag us to this fucking place when we should be re-energizing for your big fucking battle that you just HAD to slip in there right as I was about to zonk out? Explain it in a way that my puny human mind can understand, YEAH?"

I don't really know how long they've been going at it, but I step up and pull Ethan back into my arms. Last thing I want him doing is angering Fate, if that's truly who this woman is. I am continuously blown away by the fact that my boy seems to make friends and enemies from every corner of the metaphysical universe...

"Greetings Alpha Jameson," the woman says to me, completely ignoring every single thing Ethan just said to her. "Now that you're here and aware, we can begin, yeah?"

I have to restrain Blue from pouncing at her. His little psycho side is coming to the surface, not the cuddly little side. And now that the goddess isn't holding the reigns with the deal, I don't know what he'll do.

"He won't hurt me," she says as she flippantly jumps onto a rock that wasn't there two seconds ago.

"So, your nap doesn't leave me much time to explain, but here's the cliff notes, yeah?

"The deities that are the family that fucked with my prophecies and Ethan's fate are going to attack shortly after you wake up. Ethan here needs every member of his family to be able to combine all the powers in his blood to kill the bitch who started it all. The rest will fall after her with no additional input."

I'm sure my face looks like a toddler who just had calculus put in front of him... WHAT?

"Okay... I guess you need a bit more," she mutters looking to the sky. She's annoyed at us for being clueless? I'm beginning to understand why my boy was snarling.

"Long story short, these deities are not all powerful. They are just like the rest of us. They are just another type of magic being, like witches, fae, or demons. They're similar to demons where they get power from deals. They essentially take part of the essence of the individual they have a deal with for the entirety of the time the deal is in effect.

"Ethan never promised her anything except for she would get to claim the life of someone he loved if he killed. Because he got so good at NOT killing, she didn't get what she wanted."

The puzzle pieces start falling into place inside my head.

That's the reason for the power boom in my boy. The deal was broken. The goddess can't siphon from him anymore...

But what does this have to do with a battle?

"Everyone else who cut a deal with her swore their own allegiance to her. Esther actually was twice sworn, because Connor never made a vow like she promised he would.

"But the bitch gave Ethan the power to destroy her by becoming foresworn when she let her nephew kill Ethan before the babies were born... And yes, Alpha, you can kill the asswipe. You have the legal right to do so under the laws of heaven and the universe."

I growl in approval, but it feels hollow without my wolf here to back me up.

"Your wolves will do their parts, but I am not allowed to speak to them in any other plane than the waking world. It is law. I am already pushing the limits of the loopholes by bringing you here...

Ethan pulls himself from my arms and drops to the ground pouting, thumb in his mouth. I wish I could see inside his mind, but it is closed off to me in this place.

"Quit throwing a tantrum, little boy," she chuckles. The rock she's standing on just disappears and she slowly floats back down to the ground. "You need to be a grownup to finish this."

"How does me having power equal needing my family and everything else you said? You haven't said anything!" he shouts, wildly throwing his hands up in the air, narrowly missing clipping me in the nuts. "If you want me to wing it, then just fucking say so!"

I worry for this boy... He's going to get himself killed by Fate before he can *fulfill* his fate...

But she just laughs, a full-throated belly laugh that stretches on for minutes. When she finally straightens herself out, she looks years younger, even with the water in her eyes. There's a sparkle thcrc that wasn't present before.

"You make me miss being mortal, Ethan," she says with a smile.

"Fine. Here's the deets you need," she says as she crouches in front of my boy. "Get Stabby. Get a bit of everyone's blood on it, WITH THEIR BLESSING - That's very important - Then you have to plunge that into the bitch's heart while it's still beating. It has to beat for another one hundred and seventy two beats before it stops in order to completely destroy her."

<u>Ethan</u>

The fuck this bitch say? How in the hell was I supposed to go into the battle without having the "deets" as she put it.

"That's a bit more specific than anticipated," says Daddy in a much more diplomatic manner than I can possibly manage at this point.

While Daddy is taking the polite approach, I go over the list again in my head.

Blood from everyone. Who is everyone?

I'm guessing it's our family, so that would explain why I needed to get Connie and Shaun and everyone back together at the house.

Does that include Felix and Celeste? Max? The babies? Jack?

"Who all do I have to bleed to power up Stabby?" I interrupt whatever they're talking about. "I'm not cutting into my babies."

Ric looks aghast, like the thought didn't even cross his mind. Well, it sure as fuck crossed mine. I watch her eyes do that filmy thing again before she answers.

"The ones you claim as family, only those who have come of age. It does not need include any blood relations you do not claim."

Considering I have none of those left living that I'm aware of, that's a good thing... oh I guess that would count for Sully's family, but I don't claim them since I haven't met them yet... same with Dad's family.

"What about the one hundred whatever beats thing?" I ask the other question. I hope I don't need to count.

"You won't have to count. You just have to make sure she doesn't bleed out, suffocate, or die from any other means than the stab wound. It has to be the final wound on her body. Her heart will do the rest, one beat for every instance she perverted the universe's plans for her own gains."

Sheesh. I only know about the half a dozen or so she did in just my time on the planet. Bitch was fucking up *long* before that prophecy, apparently. Daddy did the math, too, cuz he just let out a low whistle and is shaking his head.

So now that there is a plan, I guess we have to go back and execute a goddess.

"What do you mean the others will fall when she does?" Daddy asks Fate. I hate calling her that because she's a person and there are two others dealing with fate, so I cut in to ask her name before she can answer his question.

Little me is impatient, whether the good boy or the psycho, patience is not my strong suit.

"You can call me Cassie if you'd like," she says with a wink. I don't get the joke, but apparently Daddy does as he nearly chokes on his surprise, setting off a coughing fit.

"As for the others in her family. As she is their chosen matri-arch, when she falls, as do all of her generation. The fate of the so-called gods is based on the power of the collective. They are immortal as long as the one who holds the power remains invincible."

At my confused look, she looks annoyed but elaborates.

"Think of Zeus, Hades, and Poseidon overthrowing Kronos. The other titans just faded into obscurity as the new generation came to power. These so-called gods are descendants of those very same types of beings. They need worshipers and souls to be more than human. They choose a leader. The leader is the key to their power.

"This bitch is their chosen leader. Any who follow her to this battle will follow her into death and obscurity. Only those who have renounced her before today will ever be more than mere humans ever again."

Daddy and I look at each other with determination. We are

killing the gods today. Any who stand against us today will either die or become human.

There is no turning back for any of us at this point.

"We're ready," I growl in a powerful voice that makes Daddy throw his shoulders back in pride. "It's time to gank a bitch!"

Between one blink and the next, I'm opening my eyes to the ceiling I'm beginning to hate.

"We really fucking need to paint this ceiling, Daddy," I groan out before I roll out of bed. Killing the gods is going to require at least three cups of magic bean juice...

TWENTY-EIGHT

Ric

Watching Ethan go around to everyone to ask for their blood is rather entertaining. He's still stuck in his little psycho mode, so it's very difficult to tell whether he's being serious or not when he suggests it will be "just a flesh wound" or holding Stabby up to his face and making a high pitched voice say "Feed Me."

He got the usual suspects that I anticipated, like Edward, Connor, Bennet, and Josh. He was gentle with waking up Shaun to ask him. When he agreed, the boy braced himself for a cut, but Ethan just rubbed the flat of the blade along the still oozing wound on Shaun's side. My bluebird, even in psycho little mode, would never hurt anyone he cares about. Gross them out? Absolutely! But he would never cause them pain.

The ones that surprised me were Max, Seb, Bastian, Celeste, and Felix. Max wasn't as much of a surprise seeing as how he's been close with Ethan since we were all kids. But Seb and Bastian didn't join the pack until we were already in South Carolina. Hell, they showed up just about two years ago, right before we got Ethan back.

Their former pack leader felt threated by two alpha wolves who had more innate authority than his son, so their mother asked for a favor. She remembered my mother from before she left for college. I couldn't say no since she begged me in the name of my mother, and I'm thankful for it. Those two have become like another set of brothers to me, just as Connor and Max had over the years.

Celeste wasn't a surprise considering she and Ethan have a joint past from their time in the lab. They still don't talk about it, but I see the haunted looks in their eyes, as well as Josh's, when they think no one is looking sometimes. Felix was a shock considering how much of a little shit he was in the spring in Atlanta. But he's definitely made up for it by now.

My wolf grumbles in my head, still upset about being left out of the planning session with Cassie. I ignore him because he will just have to go on instinct when we're out there fighting. I'm still thrown that the Fate who has taken an active role in our fight decided to name herself after the damn oracle of Delphi who defied Apollo... Come to think of it, wasn't the asshole doctor's name Delphi?

"FUCK!" I slam my fist into the wall, luckily going through only drywall to the other side. Everyone in the room stops and turns to me. Well, everyone except my boy who is looking around frantically.

"Ethan, baby?" I ask rushing over to him. Last thing we need is a meltdown or panic attack. "What's wrong? What are you looking for?"

He looks at me with terror in his eyes before he says, "We're gonna lose. She's not here!"

Ethan

Getting everyone's blood is easy enough. Each person chuckles or laughs as I try to make it as silly as possible, when in reality it's the most serious task I've ever undertaken... well, aside from giving birth. We all gather in the living room, Connor still in the chains for the time being, so that Shaun can be included in the plans. We need to make sure everyone is protected and safe and... oh...

Oh, no...

Daddy punches the wall, but that's not important. It's just drywall. That doesn't matter... What matters is Stabby isn't complete. He can't be complete.

Daddy is looking at me with worry. Everyone in the room is staring at me. "She's not here..." I repeat it over and over like somehow, she's just going to magically show up.

"Who isn't here?" someone asks from across the room.

My father takes one look at me and the surprise on his face melts to a sad smile. "My wife, Lisa."

At that moment, the sound of a car pulling up out front puts us all on alert. Bastian heads toward the door, causing Felix to run straight to the corner where the babies are. I don't know what is going on there, but now is not the time to worry about that. We all wait for a shout or something.

Max is preparing his toys that I got him for Christmas. I never really expected we would need those kinds of weapons, but when you're fighting gods, you use what you got...

I'm squeezing Daddy so tightly, I can almost hear his ribs starting to crack when a voice announces, "Someone made a wrong turn somewhere and ended up on my kitchen counter."

I push Daddy away to chuckles bounding around the room as I run to Mama Lisa. She's holding out Mr. Whiskers to me. I grab him and clutch him to my chest, wondering how in the hell he got all the way over there.

Cassie, my wolf tells me. *You dropped the toy when we shifted in front of Cassie.*

I can almost hear the Fate giggling in my head as I roll my eyes. I snatch Mr. Whiskers from Mama Lisa and then wrap her up in a hug. She has just saved the day for us all.

Everyone breaks into uncontrollable laughter when I hold up Stabby and say, "Feed Me, Seymour."

What can I say? I love musicals.

TWENTY-NINE

Ric

As soon as the tip of the blade pierces Lisa's fingertip, there's a charge to the air. We all feel the change and the chuckles stop. Even the babies stop making noise for a second. Fortunately, one of my sons knows how to lighten the mood and lets the mother of all farts rip, echoing through the silent room.

The first one to giggle is my boy and soon the whole room is holding their stomachs, tears in their eyes. It only gets worse when Felix, who is closest to the babies, starts gagging amid his laughter. The smell slowly rolls through the room and pretty much everyone except Ethan, Shaun, and Savannah are making excuses to go check on something somewhere else in the house.

"Woo, boy! Alec!" Ethan says waving his hand in front of his face. "You could give Petey a run for his money in the smell department!"

Somewhere in the hall I hear Celeste and Josh bark out a laugh. It takes a second for the memory to come to me. Pete was the man with the horrible stench that Ethan took into the basement of the old Sinclair house in Ohio.

"Don't you dare compare my godson to that piece of trash ever again!" Max's voice rings out from the front door area. "Or I'll have to confiscate Bertie and his gang for a month!"

Ethan's face is showing complete betrayal as he picks up our son to check and make sure he didn't have a blowout and it was in fact just gas. He is taking to fatherhood like he was meant for it. I can only hope we have the opportunity to raise all of our children and show them the right way to be a parent. I hope we don't fuck up our kids like our parents did with us.

In my musings, I didn't notice my boy coming toward me with our son in hand.

"I heard you haven't officially met your kids, Daddy."

The baby boy is thrust into my hands, but luckily Jack gave me plenty of practice with holding a baby. Ethan doesn't even check my comfort level before he's picking up our daughter to hand to Shaun who is still on the sofa. Last, he grabs our other son and comes to stand between us.

"You are holding Alec, the stink bomb," he giggles out. "Also the alpha and second born of the three.

"Shaun is holding Tessa Olivia, our little princess." He leans down and kisses her head, giving his best friend a nuzzle on the top of his head on the way back up. "She is also an alpha."

Lifting up our other son, he blows a raspberry on his tummy before tucking the baby back into his arms.

"This guy is our firstborn, Zander," he says sobering. "Zander is omega like me, like Jack..."

I think my eyes are going to bug out of my head. Did he just say my little brother is an omega? There's no way to know until we get our wolves if a wolf is a beta or omega. Otherwise, there would be arranged matings all over the place, bidding wars, kidnappings...

"Yes, Ric," he says pushing himself and Zander into my side for cuddles. "The ones who know what to look for know how to tell before the wolf shows up. An omega wolf will always recognize others like themselves. Your father *knew* I was an omega before my wolf came, remember?"

"I... I... I..." I have to take a few deep breaths to be able to continue. "I always thought he just said that to sweeten the deal with them. It was a fifty-fifty shot and the fae wouldn't want just another beta wolf."

Celeste comes back in the room with Jackie by her side. "They wouldn't want a beta wolf. They'd have killed a beta without remorse." She leads Jackie to the sofa and pulls Zander from Ethan's arms to put him in Jack's. My brother looks like he is going to take his uncle responsibilities very seriously.

The fae woman pulls Alec from my arms and levels the two of us with a solemn glance.

"They're almost here. It's time."

<u>Ethan</u>

Celeste's words are bouncing around in my brain. I can't settle it down. Not the stuff about the fae killing beta wolves. I knew that from when we were in the lab... But the gods are almost here and now I have to kill a goddess and try to make sure the rest of us get out alright. How do I do that?

No. Seriously. How?

"Gimme a bit of your blood and hair," Shaun says grabbing my arm suddenly. "And I need something small and plentiful that we can hand out."

Ric goes to our penny jar on the shelf and dumps out a bunch on the coffee table while I use Stabby to pierce my finger and let a drop of my blood fall onto the tabletop. I pluck out a couple strands of my hair, because let's be honest, it's difficult to pull just one. Laying them on top of the blood drop, I wait for whatever Shaun is going to do.

He's staring at Stabby instead of looking at the blood or the hair. I snap my fingers in front of his face to wake him up and he startles, making Tessa fuss a bit in his arms.

"Hold her while I do this," he says passing my daughter off to Celeste. I gotta say, the girl looks pretty good with a baby on each hip. I hope she gets over her no mate decision someday and finds a good person. She deserves happiness.

I lose a bit of time imagining Celeste and me being pregnant together and having our kids grow up together, but I come back to the present as the pennies in a pile on the table are glowing... So is Stabby. What in the ever-loving fuck?!

"I tweaked it a bit," Shaun groans in exhaustion, leaning back against the cushions. Zander reaches out from Jack's arms to touch him. My bestie just smiles at my son before turning back to us. "Hand them out to everyone on our side. We'll keep some in here as well. They are protection and should give our family a little extra oomph for fighting."

Ric and I start gathering the pennies. It's a loud affair, so I barely hear when Shaun mutters, "I just hope the extra blood on the blade doesn't come back to bite us in the ass."

Oops. I probably shouldn't have used Stabby, but he was right here. And he's still glowing, so it should be still good, right?

Ugh, I really hope so cuz I'm so ready to shank the bitch and be free of her and her family once and for all.

Max's shout echoes down the hallway. All we hear is "FIRE IN THE HOLE!" and the house is plunged into darkness. Backup generators kick on and I speed off to give a penny to all of my family and friends. We are NOT losing anyone. Bitch is going down!

THIRTY

Ric

I've seen many battles over the years, but most of the fights I've witnessed were fought in organized ways. They were planned, much like colonial era battles where each side agreed on numbers, locations, et cetera. This is not battle. This is ambush, slaughter, genocide... The gods want to wipe us out and are using unnatural weapons and means to do it.

One of the gods is lobbing literal fireballs at my house where there are babies and children and those who are incapable of fighting. This man is ignoring the warriors and going after the innocents. He needs to be stopped...

Allow me, my wolf growls before I shift and overtake him easily. I may not be able to kill him yet, but my wolf does a damn good job of ensuring no more fireballs are getting thrown. It's kind of difficult to throw something without arms...

Turning around in a circle, it's chaos from every angle. Connor's wolf is tearing through their numbers, slashing anyone who isn't part of our pack. Bennet, Edward, and I had to make sure that anyone not of my pack stays clear of him. We are trusting his wolf to recognize pack, but cannot trust him to see past that at this point... not until we end this once and for all.

Max has planted himself by the pool and continues to launch his various explosives that he got as presents from Ethan. The maniacal glee radiating from the man makes me open my snout in a wolfish grin before I turn back to the main part of the battle to see if I can locate my boy. He zoomed out to hand out the pennies, but I haven't seen him since.

Before I can locate him, I see the one man that I must destroy. No one else gets to have this one. None of us could ever figure out how Doctor Delphi got out of the cells below the vampire ware-houses. Even knowing he is a demigod, it still didn't make sense. Edward reviewed the footage and interviewed every vampire, but the asswipe was just there one second and gone the next.

He's not getting away this time, my wolf growls to me. I whole-heartedly agree.

The look on the douchebag's face as he is tackled by four hundred pounds of nightmare fuel is priceless. Shifting back, I wrap my hands around his throat, needing to watch his terror as he experiences every second of what he put my mate through on that day. I know this won't kill him completely until Ethan has done what he needs to, but it's cathartic.

Is it wrong of me to hope my boy takes longer so Daddy can play a bit longer with his prey?

Ethan

Handing out the pennies is easy. I still had more than a handful leftover even after giving them to the teenagers and others who were the last line of defense inside the house. Not knowing how powerful or important they could be, I throw some on the roof and scatter more in a circle around the house… Can't hurt, right?

The fighting that starts is pure chaos. I know violence. I know gore. I know vivisection and blood and *this* is more than I ever expected. This isn't what I know. This is abso-fucking-lutely terrifying!

I just want to find Daddy and hide away, but that's not right. I need to be a grown up. I need to put on my big boy pants…

"Find the children and bring them to me!"

I know that voice… I *hate* that voice.

"We will force another deal, or the children will die."

The bitch is going to take my babies?! Over my dead body…

The shift to wolf is unexpected since I know I have to stab her with my knife, but I guess it *would* be easier to take her down as a wolf than as the skinny twink that I am. Somehow having triplets made me lose weight that I couldn't afford to really lose, so yeah wolf form is better to start.

Before I can reach her, one of the teenagers from our pack is thrown at her feet. I stop because I recognize the girl. This girl is Sheila. She is one of Jackie's tutors slash babysitters. After the whole Jessica thing, Ric left it up to me to vet the people around Jack since he didn't trust anyone but the warriors. Sheila was one of the first to volunteer. She loves Jack…

"How old are you, child?" the goddess asks her. I can tell Sheila doesn't want to answer, but you can't refuse. I know that feeling.

"Seventeen as of yesterday," the girl snarls, hatred burning in her eyes. "You may as well kill me now. I won't be a pawn in your game. I'm terrible hostage material."

The goddess laughs and her family echoes it behind her. Most of them are fighting but there are a handful standing here with her, just watching. I can't decide if they're bodyguards or just not the front line type of gods...

"You can end this, child. Just take a deal," one of the gods says, picking at his cuticle. "Violence really serves no purpose for any of us."

"Come with me, swear yourself to me, and we all leave this place. Your friends will get to live out their lives in peace," she whispers to the girl kneeling in front of her.

Sheila looks up in disbelief. I know that feeling. The goddess comes and offers you what you want most, but doesn't reveal the fine print. She doesn't say what the catch is or how things would play out without the deal. The teen starts looking hopeful... SHIT!

I run as fast as I can and tackle the bitch, shifting back to human as soon as I have her down.

"YOU. WILL. NOT. MAKE. ANOTHER. FUCKING. DEAL. IN. MY. FUCKING. PACK!"

With each word, my fist makes contact with her face. I can feel my inner little psycho giggling at the fact that her boobs are so fake up close. Never knew a goddess would need plastic surgery...

My anger still hasn't subsided, but around me it becomes pure insanity. I won't let the bitch get away. The teenagers have spilled from the house, leaving only Celeste and Shaun to protect Jack and the babies, but judging by the way the battle has spread out, I'm glad it didn't spill into the house.

The body beneath me tries to shift and buck me off, but I'm not letting go. I reach deep into my mind to find the source of my powers. Cassie said I needed all of my family to use all of my power, so I think of each of them...

From Connor, the control of the senses comes to mind. I may not be a Sinclair by blood, but I've been in my brother's mind enough to know how his power works. I can fake it...

From my father, I will heal everything that comes my way. Through my blood and hair on the pennies, we will all heal. No one will die...

From my mother and grandmother, the souls of our departed loved ones will come to fight beside us. May the ghosts of the past haunt our enemies to their dying breaths...

From Max, I have the iron will to hold true to what is right and honest, no matter what the world throws at me. I will protect the innocent who cannot protect themselves...

From Shaun, I have the unwavering loyalty. I will never abandon this fight...

From Sully, I have the unyielding faith and hope that it will all work out in the end...

For the others, I will fight to the death in the same way I know that they would for me...

The woman beneath me keeps trying to wiggle out of my grip. The more I look at her the more I see she is just a woman. She is nothing to me, but the shell of something rotten. She is an echo of a dream...

"I will take them all from you, Ethan Lewis Sinclair!" she snarls at me as she frees an arm to take a swipe at my face. I'm kinda surprised she made contact when I feel the slight sting on my cheek. I reach up and see blood when I pull my fingers away...

From my grandfather, I have the ability to go into another's mind completely. I can pull memories or talk to them or listen in, sure... But there is a darker side to the power that I have done my best to resist the urge to use.

FUCK THAT SHIT

I release the restraints on my ability and shove myself into the mind of a millennia old woman and prepare for the backlash...

Nothing... She isn't fighting me being here...

I don't know if it's because she wasn't expecting an intrusion or if she just has zero defense against me, but I'll take it. I root around for a bit and find the core memory of her becoming the leader, the one with the power... the moment she became the Goddess with a capital G instead of the little sister.

The girl is standing before the others like her. She is trembling with nerves, but the smile on her face is pure joy. She promises she will not fail them, not like the ones who went before them...

Before I rip it away from her and end this bloody shit, I can't resist the urge. I need to let her know I'm in here and it's me. I get a perverse kind of thrill out of it when I say it. I always wanted to say it...

Hey Bitch! We've been trying to reach you about your vehicle's extended warranty...

Her eyes widen for a split second before I rip the memory to shreds. One moment in her thousands of years of life unravels it all. To stop her from going into shock and dying from that, I need to replace the shredded memories with something. It's cruel and unusual punishment, but I can think of no one more deserving...

Baby Shark, do-do-do-do-do...

Thousands of years of that song on repeat is getting planted in her brain. I watch the memories reform in fast forward. There is nothing, but a toddler song over and over and over and over...

There is nothing but madness in her eyes now. She is nothing.

She is no longer even a person. As I slide Stabby into her heart, I swear her heart is beating to the beat of the damn song.

I crossed a line.

This is no longer vengeance. This is a mercy killing. I may be a little psycho, but even *I* have my limits. And I went too damn far... Hearing the one hundred and seventy second beat followed by no more, I sigh in relief.

I don't even notice the concussive blast that knocks everyone else down. I am just trying not to cry over the body of the bitch that ruined my life.

THIRTY-ONE

Ric

The blast that knocked all of us to the ground almost dislodged my hands from Doctor Fuckwit's neck. Fortunately, he is too weak to fight back, so I resume my grip to strangle him for the third time. Something tells me this time will be final by the look of horror on his face. That blast must mean that my boy succeeded.

Daddy? He calls out to me, but it sounds like he's sad. Had we lost someone? I didn't feel it. He should be excited. We won.

Daddy, I need you. I c-c-c-can't do this by myself...

Fuck the fear in the eyes of this douchenozzle. My boy needs me. I don't play around with the man underneath me anymore and just snap his neck. Cassie said they'd be human now, so I don't need to worry about him healing.

Blue, where are you? I'll come to you. I send out while I try and pinpoint his apple spice scent on the wind. I see one of the teenagers come around the corner of the house. I think it's Sheila, but it's hard to tell with all the blood on her.

"Alpha! He's back here!" she yells out. Yeah, it is Sheila, and I'm racing to the back of the house with Max and Connor hot on my heels. If he is hurt, I'll kill every single one of these former deities just to bring them back and kill them again...

Rounding the corner, I see my bluebird. He's remarkably clean for him being in the middle of such carnage. The rest of us are absolutely coated in blood and gore, well not so much me as I only strangled someone after shifting, but the rest of our side is a literal bloody mess.

Ethan is just sitting next to the body of the former goddess, rocking back and forth, humming something.

"What is that song?" Bennet asks running to catch up to us all.

"Baby Shark," comes in unison from about twenty people all around us. The teenagers were all back here, and it looks like they had a tougher battle than any of us adults did out front. The pride and hope I have in the future of our pack just increased a million-fold.

I don't know why my boy is humming that song, but it appears to be hurting him. Kneeling in front of him, I lift his face so that I can see his eyes. They're clear. He is still with us, but he looks horrified. As he notices me in front of him, he breaks and launches himself into my arms. Holding him tight, I let him sob and cry as much as he needs to. It takes a minute to understand what he's saying, and when I do, it's a struggle not to laugh at him.

"Do you think Baby Shark on repeat for a millennia would constitute as cruel and unusual punishment?"

Connor staggers away, trying to hold back his laughter, but Max doesn't bother. He falls on his ass on top of the corpse of the goddess, his choking guffaws echoing across the yard. It's too diffi-cult to hold back anymore and where there were sounds of battle only minutes before, laughter is ringing and cleaning the energy of the pack.

Ethan

It doesn't take long for my tears to turn to giggles. The stress of the day makes slipping into full little mode very easy, especially now that the G-Lady is gone. The threats are all gone now. I let the laughter and joy surround me and it doesn't even matter that I left Stabby behind. Someone else will grab him.

Daddy carries me into the living room and sets me down on the rug that we left set up for me for TV time. The cartoons Jackie was watching work just fine for me. As long as I don't have to think anymore, I'm happy. Mr. Whiskers is placed on the floor next to me, and I get a monster hug from my little brother from behind.

Looking up, I see Daddy is holding Zander now, rocking him gently as he sleeps. Everything seems to be perfect again…

"We don't know if she'll be back, but I'll be prepared for it now."

Shaun's words don't really mean much to me at first, but it harshes my mellow or whatever it is that they say, so I feel myself coming back to being grown-ish.

"Who we talking about?" I ask the room without looking away from the television. I am kind of invested in this little dog and his family. It's surprisingly deep for a kid's show. This ain't like the stuff that was on the air when I was a kid…

Connor clears his throat from the doorway. I didn't even notice he came in, but based on his wet hair, he took the time to get a shower and clean off the blood and stuff. Actually, looking around the room, everyone is cleaned up. This show is really freaking good to have distracted me that much…

"They're talking about my mother," he says as he walks past, ruffling my hair on the way. Sitting on the opposite end of the couch from Shaun, he continues. "I say we take the reprieve and just celebrate for now. Even if the bitch is still hanging around, she's powerless without an anchor."

I nearly choke on my tongue in surprise. Did Connor - perfect, respectable, honest, boy scouts wish they could be as good as him Connor - just call his mother a bitch???

"Now THAT deserves a celebration!" Max exclaims from the doorway, holding the big cooler out to a few teens. "Let's get this party started!"

THIRTY-TWO

Ethan

The party was still going strong and had even expanded to the backyard by the time Daddy and I were completely exhausted. Someone had cleaned up all the dead bodies and took a hose or something to the yard because if you didn't know better, the only sign of anything happening was a few scorch marks on the grass. Honestly, I can't even say for certain that they even happened today.

Max has a habit of playing with his explosives near the pool when no one is around.

Looking at Ric, I decide to use the babies as an excuse to get away from the celebrations. As nice as it is to be around everyone and be happy, I want some alone time with my mate. I haven't been truly alone with him in almost a month. For the first time in a very long time, I'm feeling a need to be with him in a way that I don't remember ever being before.

Daddy? I wait until he's looking at my face before I continue... *I think I'm ready to try outside of my heat.*

I watch the thoughts flit across Ric's face. They range from confusion to shock to happiness to wariness.

I'm doing my best to not just read his mind. I can do that now, but after what I did to the G-Lady, I'm more determined than ever to not push the moral limitations of my abilities.

Doing that to her made me feel icky inside.

"Are you sure?" Ric asks me out loud. "I need this out loud, today. Are you absolutely certain that you want to try this today?"

I let the love shine through our bond. The moment he feels it is obvious, especially considering he scoops me up and races for the stairs.

A few people chuckle as I wave from being thrown over his shoulder, but mostly I'm excited to be doing this.

Finally, I'm going to feel my Daddy and remember it.

Ric

Today has been magical. First, we started the day with winning the battle against the freaking gods! Then, we partied like there was no tomorrow. And then my boy asked me to be inside him outside of his heat... Absolute magic.

Unfortunately, Ethan's PTSD didn't allow us to go much further than just my fingers before his panic set in, but he was at least wanting to try...

"I'm sorry, Daddy," he whispers into the quiet of the room. He's been silent for so long I thought he had fallen asleep on me. I resume rubbing circles on his back as I pull him in tighter to me. He is half on top of my chest now.

"For what, little bird?" I ask. He has already made me the happiest man on the face of the earth by just being here and loving me and giving me three beautiful babies and expanding my family...

I feel him start to shake, and I lift my head from the pillow to look down my body to see him. I'm only just now realizing that we didn't put any pajamas on or even underwear. This is our first time outside of his heat that we've been in bed together, both totally nude.

"I'm a broken omega, Daddy," he whimpers softly. "You need someone who can love you the right way. They broke me. I don't know if I'll ever be able to be with you without being scared..."

I pull him more fully on top of me and lift his chin so that I can look into his face.

"I don't care about any of that," I tell him, wiping the tears from his face with my thumb. "I love YOU, not the sex. If the only time I get to put my dick in you is once, maybe twice a year, so be it."

I can't decide if the choking noise is laughter or sobbing, so I just hold him a little tighter against my chest. Eventually, he settles down and again I think he's asleep, but he surprises me once more.

"Daddy?"

"Yes, Blue?"

"Did you read your ring?"

I flash back to the morning before, or was it the day before that? Whenever it was, the outside of the ring was gorgeous, but inside the engraving is perfect. "You mean where it says, Forever My Daddy?" I ask him.

He nods and looks at me for a minute before opening his mouth. "Did you read mine?"

I shake my head because his waking up interrupted me before I could get a good look. He climbs off me and goes into the bathroom. Before I can worry that I disappointed him, he's skipping back in the room with the ring box. He takes out my ring and puts it on my finger.

"Read mine and say yes, Daddy." He's practically bouncing off the bed, so I pull out his ring and angle it so the light can hit it. Somehow, he managed to get my handwriting engraved inside of his ring.

Happy tears flow from both of us as I slide the ring onto his finger. I kiss him with all the passion I have in my heart. We finally stop and I breathe the words into his mouth before we can start again...

"Forever My Psycho."

EPILOGUE

<u>*Ethan*</u>

It's been a year since the babies were born... and boy what a year it's been. Daddy finally got me to do therapy. It's online and only through a video screen for now, but Doctor Brandi says I'm making good progress. She's a lot more helpful than the other ones we tried. The guy that Ric talks to, Doctor Rawlings, is a good guy, but I discovered early on that I have a harder time talking to men about what happened to me.

It's not that they're jerkfaces or anything, but it's very difficult to open up to another man about the fact that I don't see all of it as if I was repeatedly violated by all of the men brought to the lab. Doc Rawlings just doesn't see it the same way as me. He sees it how Daddy does. Doctor Brandi understands how I look at it. If she doesn't agree, she doesn't say so. She just takes the time to let me explain my feelings and lets me know they're valid even if someone else disagrees. It has made a huge difference in my confidence, both as a mate and a papa.

As I put the last of the balloons in the room and close the door, I can't wait for the trips to wake up. I'm proud to say all three of my kids are freaking geniuses. They are little zoomie machines to the point that only Daddy, me, Sully, and Gramps can keep up with them. We are dreading the day they learn to walk, and therefore run, but for right now, it's fun to watch them crawl around.

I feel the arms wrap around my waist and I know it's Daddy. He gives a sleepy groan as he kisses the back of my neck. I almost want to drag his sexy ass back to bed, but it is too close to wake up time for Tessa and the boys won't be far behind.

"Go get your coffee, Daddy," I tell him with a kiss on his cheek.

He gives me the look my comment deserves. I am notorious for being practically feral at this hour of the day, but it's their first birthday... "I've had three cups already and Sully is on his way from campus with another run."

Ric lets out an exasperated sigh and shakes his head at me. Turning to the stairs, he calls back to me softly, "I am not carrying your caffeine crashed ass back to bed an hour into the party. This one is your fault."

His laughter fills the hallway as I stare after him in outraged shock.

Looking back at the door to the room we converted into a playroom for the trips, I start bouncing on my toes. I can't wait for the party.

Life is good. My babies are growing stronger each and every day. I get to graduate after this year of classes thanks to being able to test out of a lot of subjects and taking a few online summer courses this year. My family is healthy and whole, if not wholly together, but we're working on that.

Hey, Blue?

Daddy's voice pulls my attention away from my happy musings.

Why is your brother's motorcycle in pieces in my pool?

UGH! Will those two just fucking admit they love and need each other? I mean I don't have room to talk about healthy communication but come on. You would think my bestie and my brother would have learned from my fuck up.

I'll call Shaun. You call Connor. I'm gonna give a trip to the basement to any mother fucker who puts a damper on my babies' big day. No drama for the next twenty four hours, got it?

I hear his chuckle with my own ears, not through my head. My smile comes back easily as I prepare myself to wake up the triplets. Time for Papa to get some baby smooches...

THIS IS THE END OF ETHAN AND RIC'S STORY, BUT THE JAMESON PACK IS STILL ALIVE AND WELL AND THERE IS MORE WORK TO DO FOR FATE TO CLEAN UP HER MESS...

ABOUT THE AUTHOR

I am a dog mom living it up in the insanity that is Northeast Ohio. When I'm not documenting the exploits of the characters in my head, I'm either binge reading the works of other amazing authors or losing my voice at hockey games. I'm horribly addicted to coffee, anime, and Asian dramas in addition to building my ever-growing stuffie army. To break it down to the basics, I am a neurospicy aceflux demirom hetero cis woman middle who writes about people (mostly LGBTQIA+) finding love and purpose through unexpected means. Almost all of my stories involve some facet of BDSM, but the heart of the matter is the characters and their growth.

K.A. Bauer is the paranormal alter ego of Kate Bauer.

I guess you could say Kate lives in this reality while K.A. is in a reality where mythical creatures and magic exist and fate makes finding true love easier.

For the latest news on releases and appearances, check out my website www.authorkabauer.com

For links to all of my socials and to sign up for my newsletter, check out my linktree at https://linktr.ee/authorkabauer

I can be found on most social media sites under the username @authorkabauer

K.A. BAUER BOOKS

<u>Alpha's Little Psycho Series</u>
Alive
Holly Jolly Psycho (Novella)
Unburied
Afraid
Complete Series Omnibus

<u>Jameson Pack Series</u>
Fated Mistake
Doctor Mate
Half Mate
Learned Fate

All of my books that are not under an exclusivity clause are also available direct from my store
www.authorkabauer.shop

KATE BAUER BOOKS

<u>Manor Drive Series</u>
A Little Discovery
Drag Me Up
Pet Project
Teddy Tea Time
Night Shift
No Pain, No Gain

<u>Wrenshaw University Series</u>
Freshman Fifteen
Injured Reserve
Professor's Pet
Too Many Men

<u>MR DRAG Series</u>
Wish Upon DeStarr

DOCTOR MATE

JAMESON PACK

An Alpha's Little Psycho Spin-off

Read on for a sneak preview into the continuation of the story. Ethan and Ric might have told their story, but there are many more members in the Jameson Pack.

CONNOR

Trying to sleep in a tiny ass recliner in a hospital room is not my idea of a good time. The plan was to have Ric take over so I could let my wolf out for a bit. The anger and guilt and everything are just eating me up inside and I need to release it somehow before some innocent bystander suffers. But of course, my best friend took one look at the bloody mess that was my little brother and he took off. They called him in to keep *me* from losing it, and he ran away... *just like his bitch-ass father.*

I take a few deep breaths to calm myself down. I don't know if it's the breathing exercise or if it's the barely there scent that's been coming and going all day getting stronger. I still can't quite identify exactly what it might be, but it's finally distracting enough that my wolf takes notice of it and stops fighting to come out. I am about to go to the hall to see if I can locate the source when the lights start flickering.

That's the last thing I need to deal with. Right now, Ethan is relying on machines to function in place of his organs while they regrow. His heart already stopped twice on the way here, and I don't think I could handle it happening a third time in my presence. Supposedly a witch on staff is going to swing by to check on us. They provided a moonstone with some calming properties earlier, so I would assume they'd come to collect something so valuable. But so far, only the orderly has been by to check on us since we were brought to this ward...

The lights stop flickering after a moment. I feel the need to find the scent again, but it's gone by the time I get to the hallway. I hear the rumble of an old engine desperately in need of a tune up and head over to the window. If I had a choice in my life, I could be fixing a car like that... an Impala from the looks of it...

I watch the taillights fade into the night and a part of me wishes I had the courage to admit to my Alpha that I don't want to be his Beta. My dream is long dead, though. It died the same night my family did.

A whimper from the bed pulls me to Ethan's side. Looking down at him, I have to remind myself that my whole family did not die that night... The doc said it will likely be days, if not weeks, before he wakes up and is coherent. As long as he wakes up, I can wait forever...

"I'm so sorry, little brother," I whisper as I push the bright red waves away from his face. "I'm so sorry. Shaun was right. I should have listened to your best friend. Please just wake up and I'll give you anything you want..."

Please don't hate me. I hate myself enough for us both...